CULT of the CORPSES

by
MAXWELL HAWKINS

Off-Trail Publications

Elkhorn, California

Thanks to the ambassador of voodoo fiction.
You know who you are.

Cover art by Rudolph Belarski, excerpted from *Thrilling Detective*, January 1936.

CULT OF THE CORPSES
By Maxwell Hawkins
Copyright © 2008, Off-Trail Publications
ISBN-10: 1-935031-05-8
ISBN-13: 978-1-935031-05-5

OFF-TRAIL PUBLICATIONS
2036 Elkhorn Road
Castroville, CA 95012
offtrail@redshift.com

Printed in the United States of America
First printing: December 2008

CONTENTS

Weirdness and the Detective Pulp
By John Locke

I
THE FICTION

IN THE INTRODUCTION TO *The Weird Detective Adventures of Wade Hammond: Volume 4* (Off-Trail, 2008), we attempted to document the role that Paul Chadwick's Hammond stories played in the evolution of the Weird Menace genre. They came at a time when the short-lived era of gang fiction was fading from popularity. The publisher of the Hammond stories, *Detective-Dragnet Magazine*, appeared to be phasing in detective stories with a weird element at the same time they were reducing their allegiance to the gangster. The first Hammond story, "Depths of Doom," appeared in the September '31 issue. A story we cited as an interesting example of *Detective-Dragnet's* shift was "Cult of the Corpses" (January '31), a tale that promised to put gangsters in conflict with a voodoo cult, thus combining the descendant genre with the ascendant. With such an unusual premise, the story cried out to be resurrected, and this book was born.

The author of "Cult" was Maxwell Hawkins, a name that sounds like one of the glib pseudonyms pulp authors hid their prodigious output behind, but Maxwell Hawkins was indeed an authentic name, and not a million-word-a-year-man's alter ego. But more on Mr. Hawkins in Part II.

Both Hawkins and Chadwick fueled an industry-wide trend in the pulps toward blending detective stories with weird elements. Certainly, that approach was not original to the pulps, or to that moment in time, but there clearly was a change underway in the early '30s, and that's what we will explore here.

The first problem is one of definition: what might we mean by "weird"? The dictionary allows interpretations varying from the merely odd to the outright supernatural, a wide latitude, indeed. "Weird" is a term with malleable meaning that has much to do with the person employing it. As invective, it often cloaks a mere accusation of nonconformity, as in (child to parent) "You're weird!"

Of course, criminals, the dark soul of crime fiction, constitute a special class of nonconformist, violating society's norms in violent and destructive ways. But breaking the law, itself, shouldn't be considered weird since crime is an inherent part of society, an accepted aspect of human behavior; an overhead, in business terms.

Most crime fiction teases the reader with the mysterious, posing questions like Who is the murderer? and Where did the money go? While the mystery remains unsolved, a constellation of seemingly unconnected clues hints of inexplicable, fantastic events lying just out of grasp, that suggestion of the uncanny we feel when we lose our bearings in the dark. We may pity the reader to some extent when at last the mystery is solved, the clues assembled into a coherent mass, with any sense of weirdness stripped away to reveal the inescapable logic of the universe. But mystery alone doesn't seem enough. No, it takes some special, heightened quality to achieve a state of true weirdness.

The pulp editors, in the early '30s, didn't help with a definition. They were much more vague in what they were seeking, and weren't consciously developing new genres. Editors *were* specific when they knew what they wanted. As early as the November '33 issue of *Writer's Digest*, Popular Publications editor Rogers Terrill made a stab at defining what would come to be known as Weird Menace. He fleshed out his definition for the January '35 issue, expanding it to over 400 words. He said, in part:

> To describe accurately the emotional effect we seek in *Terror Tales* and *Dime Mystery*, it is first necessary to make clear the difference between horror and terror. *Horror* is the emotion we feel when we see something hideous, gruesome, sordid; something that we find extremely disgusting or revolting. *Terror* is the emotional effect produced by extreme *fear*; it is horror brought home to us personally, the knowledge of something horrible about to happen to us or to someone dear to us, and which menace we are almost powerless to combat.

In continuing, Terrill outlined the potential role of the supernatural in the stories, the use of sadism, and other issues. He noted that detective heroes or characters were *not* welcome. His definition was obviously the result of much thought and development at that point; and, like most of the solicitations in the writers' magazines, was aimed at generating freelance submissions. In the early '30s detective pulps, which began to offer weird stories as a *portion* of their content, private communication with a handful of known writers would have sufficed to address the need. Thus, it would be fruitless to propose a strict definition of weirdness for the earlier period when neither the editors nor the writers were attempting to fulfill one. However, we can speak in terms of weird story elements that come into play.

For instance, the supernatural. While there's no law of letters that says detective stories can't have genuinely supernatural elements, it's generally absent from detective fiction. There's something about the rational conclusion that seems inextricably bound to the detective genre. Exceptions abound, of course. An early supernatural detective series in the pulps features a character named Semi-Dual, by J.U. Giesy and Junius B. Smith. Dual is a Persian mystic in America who uses astrology and other occult methodologies to solve crimes and thwart criminals. His adventures begin with "The Occult Detector," a three-part serial in *The Cavalier* (February 17 - March 2, 1912). A great number of novelettes and serials were eventually published in the Munsey and Street & Smith pulps. The series culminated with a 1934 *Argosy* serial.

Weird Tales would be an obvious place to look for weird detective stories in the '20s. In its early days (1923-24), *WT* had a companion magazine from the same company, Rural Publishing, titled *Detective Tales* (later *Real Detective Tales*). A solicitation for *WT* in the May '23 *WD* noted that, "*Weird Tales* will feature strange and unusual stories—the kind of stories that are commonly denied admission to most magazines." Magazines like *Detective Tales*, in other words. Rural, by the creation of two magazines, segregated the supernatural from the detective behind separate covers, unlike the early *Black Mask* which, unsuccessfully, contained both genres in one magazine. Throughout the '20s, solicitations for *WT* specifically barred detective stories. The obvious exception was the popular Jules de Grandin, a psychic investigator who appeared in over ninety stories from 1925-51. But they all came from the pen of a single author, Seabury Quinn, and he, seemingly, absorbed the bulk of *WT's* "detection budget."

As *WT* barred detective stories in the '20s, so did detective pulps bar the supernatural, as evidenced by these solicitations. *Black Mask* (*WD*, April '28): "We desire . . . swift moving, plausible stories of action, with plot and character interest, without the gruesome, the unnatural or supernatural." *Detective Fiction Weekly* (*WD*, November '29): "No supernaturalism." The fact that the editors stated these prohibitions suggests that they may have been receiving such unwelcome material. Edwin Baird, editor of *Detective Tales* and *Real Detective Tales*, contributed a 13-part monthly series, "How to Write a Detective Story," to *The Author & Journalist* (December '29 - December '30). In Part 12, "The Horror Story," he described the markets for detective stories and weird stories, but reaffirmed the segregation made clear by Rural (and himself, as editor) in 1923:

> Just as all magazines—or almost all—now use detective stories, so all of them sometimes use . . . tales of horror. There is, however, a wide difference in their requirements. The detective magazines—of which there are more than a dozen at this writing—insist that such stories have logical solutions. Ghosts and such are out like a light. The weird magazines, on the other hand—and I believe there are

now two or three of these—are just as insistent that their supernatural stories *be* supernatural. That is, they don't want their ghosts explained away as waggish fellows clad in bedsheets and pillowslips—they want them really to be ghosts.

However, a story can be weird absent the supernatural. Another element is the weird criminal, and there have been no shortage of these in popular fiction. The dime novels were full of them. What makes a criminal weird? One aspect may be megalomaniacal ambition. The obvious candidate is Dr. Fu Manchu, Sax Rohmer's celebrated character who appeared in thirteen books from 1913-59, and was also reprinted in popular magazines, including the pulps. Fu Manchu spawned many Oriental imitations, like A.E. Apple's Mr. Chang, who appeared many times in *Detective Story Magazine* from 1919-31. In '30s pulps, the torch was carried by the pulps *The Mysterious Wu Fang* (1935-36) and *Dr. Yen Sin* (1936). Oriental villains earn the mantle of weirdness much easier than European counterparts, owing no doubt to the degree of cultural difference between the East and West. Chinese Tongs in American cities seem weirder than Italian gangs like The Black Hand, though they may have been equal in ruthlessness. The Tongs appeared in the dime novels, and then in the pulps. In the pulps, to whom no idea was too good to run into the ground, Oriental villains became so commonplace, editors had to turn them away. For instance, Carl Happel, editor of *Two-Books Detective Magazine*, wrote in the March '34 *A&J*: "We believe that the Fu Manchu type of Chinese villain has been overdone, and also the fiendish doctor murderer; we'd rather see other types of villains, for a change." His comments didn't stop a fiendish doctor murderer from getting his own magazine in 1935: *Doctor Death*.

Other weird criminals could include people in thrall to weird beliefs. These might include devil worshippers, Thuggees, or, in the case of "Cult of the Corpses," practitioners of voodoo. These kind of groups became the lifeblood of Weird Menace. "Dealers in Death," the other Hawkins *Detective-Dragnet* story included here, involves another kind of weird criminal, one who uses eccentric means of murder, one for whom mere bullets and knives are a crashing bore. Bizarre forms of murder and torture would become the soul of Weird Menace, highlighted on virtually every cover.

Weirdness, in criminals, seems somehow natural, given that that criminals are nonconformists to begin with. The detective hero, a law enforcer, ultimately a defender of the established order, comes to weirdness a little more uneasily. One path to weirdness comes through the use of disguises. Characters in disguise are a staple of literature; it's a convenient plot device for a variety of reasons. In crime fiction, how better to move the hero through criminal circles, and hear things unavailable through conventional methods? It worked for Sherlock Holmes. Disguising oneself as a street bum or a hoodlum to gain entry to the underworld doesn't seem quite weird enough, though. Donning a flamboyant costume in order to right a wrong or strike fear in the heart of one's enemies is another question. Sampson writes extensively of characters like these in *Yesterday's Faces: Volume 3: From the Dark Side* (Bowling Green University Popular Press, 1987). *Detective Story* featured many costumed avengers throughout the '20s, most of them the inventions of Johnston McCulley. Most of them weren't detectives, technically speaking, but criminals acting altruistically. Bi-legal, perhaps. McCulley's costumed characters included The Thunderbolt (1920-21), who wore a black hood with a lightning bolt on the forehead; The Man in Purple (1921), who dresses as you might expect, with purple mask, too; The Crimson Clown (1926-31), scary in a silk clown suit; and others. All worked in extralegal, vigilante fashion, but, then, what official police department would ever sanction a professional to operate in such a manner? All of these characters laid the groundwork for The Shadow, The Spider, and the other eccentric pulp heroes of the '30s.

Outside the characters are settings and atmosphere. An "old, dark house," a remote castle, or an abandoned vessel in the fog, can heighten a story's weirdness, as can the proverbial "dark and stormy night," or a wind whistling through a graveyard. Anything that makes the world seem somehow . . . haunted.

And, with that, let's end this cursory overview of what must be an encyclopedic subject, weirdness in the detective story.

Weirdness, we can conclude, was an occasional presence in detective pulps from about the beginning of such things. However, it's not until the early '30s that active solicitation of weirdness by the editors becomes apparent as a trend. A contributing factor may have been the proliferation of new titles from the late '20s forward. Whereas, previously, a few magazines catered to the mainstream, now the market was increasingly split between a greater number of magazines, and crafting a pulp toward a smaller—but not too small—niche made more sense.

The first solicitation we have located *in favor of* a weird-detective slant comes from Fawcett's *Startling Detective Adventures*, a bedsheet that debuted with a December '29 issue date. It combined true-crime articles with detective fiction. Its solicitations for the fiction, such as this one, emphasized its special flavor:

> It is preferred to have a detective as the hero. As the title implies, stories must contain exciting action in a weird and bizarre atmosphere. The magazine does not, however, use weird or mysterious stories which have not a detective slant. [*A&J*, November '29]

Clayton, in this period, published *Clues* and introduced a new title, *All Star Detective Stories* (first issue, October '29). Carl Happel, editor of both magazines, stated his wants for both in the February '30 *WD*: "detective, underworld and mystery stories that are rational and real, devoid of fantasy or weirdness." In the December '30 issue, he restated: "We use almost every kind of crime and mystery except those wherein the supernatural, pseudo-scientific or fantastic play a part." Fast forward to 1933. *All Star Detective* was history, there were many more detective titles on the newsstands, and *Clues'* editors were in rebellion against the pulp's former policies. In the March '33 *A&J*, editor T.R. Hecker was quoted as finding it difficult to get "good horror stuff." He wanted variety for the magazine, but "action must take the place of deduction. The thrill and horror elements are especially wanted in novelette lengths; more of the unusual in short lengths." Later in the year, *Clues* was purchased by Street & Smith with F. Orlin Tremaine as new editor. He stated his preferences as: "Weird and horror elements are permitted, but the horror should be played down" (*A&J*, September); and *Clues* is "a wide-open market for good short-stories of the detective type, with a preference for horror and weird elements in their development." These solicitations for *Clues* represent the most clear-cut renunciation of the past—as opposed to new companies and magazines that started anew in this period.

One of the dynamic, new companies was Popular Publications, which debuted with four pulps having October 1930 cover dates, one of which was *Detective Action Stories*. The word "action" in the title was code to indicate a distinction between modern, action-oriented stories and traditional deductive or mystery fiction. *Detective Action* favored vigorous stories, but never solicited weird elements. When the much more successful *Dime Detective* debuted from Popular in November '31, the distinction with *Detective Action* was slight: "stories must contain an adequate amount of action and mystery, although the action need not be so heavily stressed as in *Detective Action Stories*." Less than a year later, *Dime's* policy had been modified: "We want detective stories of mystery and action with a slight horror twist. Emphasis, however, must be on the mystery" (*WD*, September '32). In the following issue of *WD*, editor Harry Steeger expanded on the formula:

> So if you have a flair for the menace and horror angle of detective-action stories and can hold the thrills through anywhere from 10,000 to 15,000 words, you might find a good steady market here. Don't submit any deductive detective tales. The shadow of horror to come must be cast darkly over every page. And things must move along rapidly. Unusual characters help, also.

And in November 1933's *WD*: "*Dime Detective* . . . stresses the *menace* type of mystery . . . You can use a slight twist of horror angle, but it must be explained logically in the end. Be plausible! Don't try out-and-out horror for this publication."

By this time, Popular was already offloading the horror into more specialized titles. *Dime Mystery Book* (first issue, December '32) started out as a magazine for simultaneous magazine and book publication of novel-length stories. The initial solicitation stated: "the story must have better than average dramatic values, these to be obtained either through conflict, menace, or the horror element. In short, they must pack thrills as well as mystery" (*WD*, November '32). After ten issues, the book approach was dropped and the pulp changed title to *Dime Mystery Magazine*. Editor Rogers Terrill's new emphasis was paraphrased by *WD*:

> They are going to accentuate horror stories, ranging from pseudo-scientific theme through the gamut of horror to werewolf and vampire types. These will include stories of eerie menace laid against a background of weird threats, the succession-of-mysterious-murder type, the frightened girl in the old dark house type, the Asiatic menace (preferably transported to this country). As Rogers Terrill . . . says, "In short, anything that gives readers plenty of chills and thrills. We are going to strive for variety in horror, and authors should try particularly to make stories read convincingly. We don't want readers to say, 'That couldn't happen!' No matter how grotesque, there must be logical motivation. There is also a special need for a few shorts of five thousand words which feature the clever crime-fighter à la The Gray Seal." [*WD*, August '33]

In the following issue of *WD*, Terrill elaborated:

> Horror is our stock in trade, and it must be realistically and convincingly done. We want the off-trail story—something which gets away from the usual stock themes and characters. The pseudo-scientific story of the madman's laboratory will be used only in those cases where the author has managed to develop an original plot theme and a brand new slant on the mad doctor. Stories of black magic and werewolfery will be used only in cases where the author through bona fide research has sufficiently familiarized himself with the subject to produce convincingly interesting reading. Stories of impossible adventures on other planets are not wanted. [*WD*, September '33]

The pattern that emerges is that Popular responded to the weird-detective trend by making that an emphasis of *Dime Detective* and then, with the creation of *Dime Mystery*, began to resegregate the detective and the weird into separate magazines. A February '34 *WD* solicitation for *Dime Detective* makes no mention of outré elements: "Soft-pedal the deduction treatment. Accentuate the mystery and action. Get unusual situations. Build up more realism. And keep in mind that there are taboos on the gangster, racketeer and secret service." The weird-detective element found a better home in *The Spider* (first issue, October '33); whereas, *Dime Mystery* was joined, in the name of purveying the weird, by *Terror Tales* (first issue, September '34) and *Horror Stories* (first issue, January '35). And, at that point, Weird Menace was a fully-emerged genre.

At Standard Magazines, another new house, the flagship was *Thrilling Detective*. Its May '33 *WD* solicitation read, in part, "No supernatural, sex, mystic, or 'monster' stories wanted." But, by that time, they were well into Perley Poore Sheehan's Doctor Coffin series (June '32 - September '33), which featured a former character actor turned mysterious crime-fighter who ran a string of funeral parlors for a day job. No, not supernatural or mystic, but well within weird-detective parameters, if not the exemplar of the breed. This reminds us again that the solicitations only applied to stories being sought from the freelancing public, and not necessarily the entire magazine which filled some of its content in private arrangements with authors and agents. *The Shadow*, for example—spawned from the mysterious announcer of a radio show, itself spawned from *Detective Story Magazine*—only solicited the straight and narrow: "We want detective stories which are interesting as well as active. . . . A purely deductive story is not wanted, but one with a judicious mixture of deduction, action, and danger will always hit the spot" (*WD*, May '33). All the weirdness of the detective (and the criminal) would come from Walter Gibson's lead novels.

When Standard issued a companion magazine, *Popular Detective* (first issue, November '34), the formula varied from *Thrilling Detective's*: "We will use all types of crime, mystery and detective stories. Also an occasional bizarre, weird or horror story" (*WD*, November '34).

Dell's *All Detective* (first issue, November '32) featured the offbeat from its inception:

> *All Detective* is especially interested in stories with unique and different ideas. . . . The purely deductive story is not wanted, neither is the gang drama. Stories with glamour, strong suspense, startling development, their setting in unusual and out-of-the-way places, get a fast reading and checks. Unusual crime methods, accompanied by a well-characterized hero, a logical solution of mystery, and a dramatic plot, will ring the bell every time. Horror and exotic stories are used occasionally. [*A&J*, January '33]

Editor Carson Mowre added an emerging codeword for a subsequent description: "The 'menace' type of detective story is now being favored" (*WD*, September '33). "Menace" indicated paranoia-inducing suspense the way "action" had come to stand for flying fists, gunplay, and car chases. Earlier in the year, agent Lurton Blassingame had attempted a definition of "menace":

> There is an unusually good market today for the well-written story of menace. If this word does not give you a clear picture of the type of fiction desired, I suggest that you read *The Phantom of the Opera* and the adventure of Sherlock Holmes in which he uncovers *The Hound of the Baskervilles*. Then to get a little closer to the present, reread Sax Rohmer's *Fu Manchu* and you will be ready to read current magazines with a full understanding of what editors mean when they speak of "menace." In this type of story some person or thing hangs a veil of horror over the characters in the story; we never know when this "menace" will strike, but we do know it will continue to commit depredations until the hero does his stuff and overcomes it in the final climax. *Dracula* was a menace play. ["Why Aren't Your Detective Stories Selling?," *WD*, May '33]

Mowre continued to amplify his requirements: "Make your ideas as unusual and outstanding as possible. And keep to the action type of detective work. Nobody seems to like the easy-chair detective these days. Blood and thunder, menace and murder are the rule" (*WD*, January '34). He later arrived at a definition of his needs for the magazine that made clear, in contrast to the cerebral appeal of the traditional detective story, the new kind of story was aimed dead-on at the emotions:

> Menace is the strongest method of creating suspense. Draw the antagonists of the hero as such resourceful, diabolical characters that the reader fears the outcome; draw the crimes of the antagonists so vividly, stressing the physical horror, that fear of this fate grows in the reader. Make him *feel* the crime, not as plot development, but as the ghastly reality. Color helps suspense: characters and situations which in themselves are exciting to the emotions. The bizarre is another aid: freakish, monstrous, fantastic criminal actions given an aspect of plausibility. Criminal actions which could but don't happen. Avoid the stock in character and situation. [*A&J*, April '34]

All Detective lasted two years and three months. Late in the run, the pulp ran stories featuring a weird villain, Doctor Death. *All Detective* changed title to *Doctor Death* and the pulp folded after three more issues.

Other magazines participated in the weirdness movement, sometimes briefly. *Scotland Yard*, a Dell pulp, signed on early. Among the possibilities for submissions, editor Richard A. Martinsen included, "Mystery or horror stuff—grand—where the sleuth makes good" (*A&J*, October '30). *Illustrated Detective* was a Tower magazine, sold exclusively at Woolworth's and aimed at female readers. It used "a considerable number of . . . stories that bring in psychic phenomena that may or may not exist" (*WD*, July '32). *Detective*, an odd-format pulp that lasted three issues, asked for "Plenty of horror and plenty of menace built into a detective yarn" (*Writer's Review*, January '34). Even *Weird Tales* caved in eventually, running stories like Arthur B. Reeve's "The Death Cry" (May '35), to howls of reader protests; a weird detective story—with a rational conclusion—was not a weird tale as far as they were concerned. In the March '36 *WD*, editor Farnsworth Wright listed "sensational detective mysteries that are essentially weird and crammed with action" among the many types of unusual fiction he would accept.

The apotheosis of the early '30s trend was a pulp that made weird detective fiction its banner medium: *Strange Detective Stories*. It came from the publisher of *Nickel Detective*, a skeletally-thin, 5¢ pulp that otherwise gave no hint of weirdness. *Nickel Detective* ran for six issues from January-August, 1933. After a two-month hiatus, the company issued the full-size pulp, *Strange Detective Stories*, seemingly a bandwagon jump, to embrace that which *Nickel* had eschewed. *Strange Detective* lined up name authors to inaugurate the magazine, and then failed after four issues, so it never became much of a freelance market. But, while optimism reigned, editor Ralph Daigh laid out an enticing formula:

> *Strange Detective Stories* makes its bid with more imaginative blood-and-thunder than is featured by the old-line publications. Stories should be strange even to the point of weirdness. There must naturally be a detective hero, though he may be a private investigator or the like. Avoid a deductive solution tied up in the last few paragraphs and the so-called surprise ending. [*A&J*, November '33]

With talented authors like Robert E. Howard, Erle Stanley Gardner, Hugh B. Cave, and E. Hoffmann Price, it's demise was a tragedy. No doubt, the all-star lineup made the magazine too expensive to produce in the tough penny-a-word market of the Depression. Popular Publications revived the concept as *Strange Detective Mysteries* in late '37, giving new life to weird detective stories independent of the hero and Weird Menace genres.

Where do the two Maxwell Hawkins stories collected here fit in? When A.A. Wyn took over Magazine Publishers from Harold Hersey in late '29, one of the titles he inherited was *The Dragnet Magazine*, a prototype of the gang pulp. Hersey went off to form his chain of overt gang pulps, *Gangster Stories*, *Racketeer Stories*, etc. When Hersey ran afoul of the censors in early '30 for promoting gangsterism in his magazines, Wyn, seemingly to avoid become embroiled in the controversy, changed the title of *The Dragnet* to *Detective-Dragnet Magazine*. After some months, other types of detective fiction were brought into *Detective-Dragnet*. Hawkins' novelettes appear to have been the first with a truly weird element, appearing in the January and July, 1931, issues, pioneering contributions to the weirdness movement. Both were prominently featured, both as lead novels and illustrated on the front cover. The Wade Hammonds began appearing in September '31, and grew in weirdness as they went along. Future Doc Savage author, Lester Dent, began appearing with a series of weird detective stories, starting with "The Sinister Ray" in the March '32 issue.

By late '31, the vague outlines of the new direction had been sketched out by Wyn, which August Lenniger characterized in his December '31 *WD* article, "New Horizons for Mystery Stories":

> [Wyn] is featuring, and calling for a new type of detective adventure story in which atmosphere plays an important part; in which the writer can unlimber his imagination within reasonable bounds. . . . First and last, Mr. Wyn wants a mystery story: a baffling, unusual, but realistic crime or insidious threat with attempts at solution or frustration that key the reader to a high pitch of breathless suspense. . . . Use your imagination! There are plenty of interesting ways of killing people that haven't yet been tried. . . . [Chadwick's "The Curse of Kut-Amen"] depends for at least fifty percent of its interest upon the weird atmosphere which the author has cleverly woven into his plot.

In a November '32 *A&J* solicitation blurb, Wyn was more specific:

> *Detective-Dragnet* prefers a sinister note in its detective stories. A woman interest also is required. It will consider stories with an apparently supernatural background, although the weird elements should be explained in a natural manner.

Detective-Dragnet's last issue was December '32. After a two-month break, it reemerged as *Ten Detective Aces*. Lester Dent's stories continued appearing through the end of 1933. Chadwick's Wade Hammond ended up appearing 39 times through 1936. Wyn continued to ask for a touch of the weird: "*Ten Detective Aces* will use 'dramatic detective and mystery stories with a sinister note' " (*A&J*, March '33); "*Ten Detective Aces* wants unusual stories with heavy emphasis on the quality of menace overhanging the action-detective plot" (*WD*, May '34); "The menace-action type story is one of the best for us. . . . horror stories, stories from the murderer's point of view . . ." (*WD*, October '34).

Our conclusion, from this preliminary examination of the topic, is that weird elements have been an inherent part of detective fiction; that they appeared in the pulps in the teens and '20s; that publishers, for the most part, segregated detective and weird fiction; but that, in the early '30s, as pulp titles began to proliferate, some detective pulps began to feature weird detective fiction; and, in time, other genres, like the hero pulps and Weird Menace, emphasized weird elements to the degree that most detective pulps returned to featuring predominately straightforward crime fiction.

II

THE AUTHOR

MAXWELL ALLEN HAWKINS, known as "Max," was born September 30, 1895 in Burlington, Iowa, a city on the Mississippi River that looks across the water to Illinois. He was the son of Helen W. and Albert B. Hawkins, the youngest of three children. His sister, Edith, was older by twelve years, and his brother, Kenneth, by ten.

We know nothing of his early years until he entered Harvard in 1914. His hometown then was listed as Chicago. The *Harvard University Register* of 1916 lists a number of activities and clubs for him, including the Social Service Entertainment Committee, the Speakers Club, and the Harvard Dramatic Club. As a member of the Harvard University Boat Club, he was coxswain on a sophomore crew that set a new interclass record over one-and-seven-eighths miles in beating archrival Yale on Boston's Charles River Basin. He had a summer job in Chicago after his sophomore year, as a navigation inspector for the U.S. Commerce Department, Bureau of Navigation. During his senior year, he served on *The Harvard Lampoon's* Board of Editors. He graduated with a degree in journalism.

Harvard's Military Record in the World War, published by The Harvard Alumni Association in 1921, lists the war records of thousands of alumni, most submitted by the individuals themselves. Hawkins' entry reads:

> Hawkins, Maxwell Allen, c '14-'18. Enrolled coxswain U.S. Naval Reserve Force April 25, 1917; assigned to Scout Patrol N. 587; discharged January 1, 1918 for physical disability.

The term "coxswain" doesn't imply that Hawkins was racing for Uncle Sam against the Boche; coxswain also indicates someone in charge of navigating small watercraft. The lengthy and evocative boat-chase scene in "Dealers in Death" adds to the evidence he was well-schooled in boating. "Dealers" also includes a reference to boxing, and a knowledgeable reference to track and field: "Ted Trask had covered the four-forty on the cinder track in forty-nine seconds." That would have been a national-class collegiate time when "Dealers" was published. Hawkins had probably been a good athlete, and remained a sports fan.

If Hawkins had made it overseas during the war, his entry would have revealed it. Therefore, the following comment by the detective Spayne, in "Cult of the Corpses," does not derive from Hawkins' personal experience:

> "I was a couple of blocks down on Broadway, when I heard that machine gun to stutter. You couldn't fool me on the sound. I'd heard it too often in France."

"Cult" demonstrates detailed knowledge of Haiti and voodoo. Hawkins explained the genesis of the story in a letter published in the same issue of *Detective-Dragnet* (reprinted in full in this volume). His interest in voodooism had been sparked by some of the older men he met in his brief Navy service. In "Cult," the hero, Ben McCray, justifies his own insights:

> "I was, at one time, a second looey in the Marines. Went into Haiti in 1915. That's when President Guillaume Sam was assassinated— or rather butchered, because the enraged people of Port-au-Prince literally tore him limb from limb."

The historical facts are accurate. The Marines occupied Haiti from 1915-34; President Sam's fate was as McCray so colorfully describes.

Hawkins married the former Anne Bishop, date unknown. They had a daughter, Anne (born in Newark, 1937), and a son, John K. Hawkins. John served in the Marines, duration unknown.

We lack information on Maxwell Hawkins' activities during the '20s, but obituaries list the various newspapers he worked on in his career: the *Kansas City Post*, the *Milwaukee Sentinel*, the *New York Journal*, the *New York Post*. When he died, October 4, 1962, age 67, he was a copy editor for New York's *Daily News*, where he had worked since 1950. It was his third stint with the *Daily News*.

His first known pulp stories appear in early '30, under the name Maxwell A. Hawkins. There were two in *Detective Fiction Weekly* (January 4, February 15); and a third in the January issue of *The Underworld Magazine* ("Caught by a Hair," described on the TOC as "a back-stage tragedy"). Thereafter, he dropped the middle initial from his byline.

His next known appearance was "Cult of the Corpses." This collection includes his only two *Detective-Dragnet* stories. The bulk of his pulp publications appear from 1930-37. He ended up with seventeen appearances in *Detective Fiction Weekly* in that period; also, with sixteen in *Dime Detective*, starting with the second issue (December '31). He made scattered appearances in *Argosy*, *Complete Detective Novel Magazine*, *Thrilling Detective*, *Popular Detective*, and *Ace-High Detective*. He had only a handful of detective stories published after '37.

He was quick to the mark in selling *Dime Sports* a rowing story for their first issue (July '35). No doubt, his acquaintance with Harry Steeger, editor of *Dime Detective*, and head of Popular Publications, made it an easy sell. All told, he sold at least seven shorts to *Dime Sports* through 1941. Most, if not all, take rowing as their subject.

The vast majority of Hawkins' published stories appear to be shorter works, unlike these two *Detective-Dragnet* tales, which were lead novels. Judging from the relatively small number of stories he published, his pulp career may have amounted to little more than a hobby. Of his 58 known stories (there are likely to be more sports stories), here is the breakdown by year:

1930	3	1940	0	1950	1
1931	5	1941	4		
1932	10	1942	1		
1933	7	1943	0		
1934	8	1944	2		
1935	8	1945	0		
1936	3	1946	0		
1937	3	1947	0		
1938	2	1948	0		
1939	0	1949	1		

If creative writing had been a hobby, it became a little more than that in late '35. With a co-writer, Bertrand Robinson, Hawkins sold a play, *Crime Marches On*, to Broadway producers. In news reports, Hawkins is identified as a "former newspaper man," but not as a pulp writer. The play went into rehearsal in September. The lead male role, a poet, went to Elisha Cook Jr., best remembered now as Wilmer, the gunsel, in the 1941 film of *The Maltese Falcon*. The lead female, in her first major role, was the late Will Rogers' 18-year-old daughter, Mary Rogers. The story involved a Tennessee hick who wins the Pulitzer Prize for Poetry; he ends up versifying on a radio show; the resulting mayhem turns into a murder mystery. The show opened Wednesday, October 23, 1935. Brooks Atkinson, the *New York Times* reviewer, was somewhat less than amused:

> *Crime Marches On*, which was acted at the Morosco last evening, raises a cosmic question. What is fun? To Bertrand Robinson and Maxwell Hawkins, who wrote what they describe as a melodramatic farce, and Edward Clarke Lilley, who staged it, fun is an ear-splitting fandango in the booby-hatch, mixing good satiric lines with police court horror. Many people in last night's audience appeared to hold the same opinion. Although this courier rose spontaneously to the promiscuous low comedy gibes at radio's good name and the administration, *Crime Marches On* impressed him as a drama that shouted itself out of existence before the evening was over. Gentler and funnier would be a suitable admonition to the rogues who swept up this comic improvisation into the dust-pan of the stage. Fun is fun, as teacher says, but yelling is only a dream play.

The United Press review praised the players but not the play: "[*Crime Marches On* misses.] The fault lies in the story itself and authors Bertrand Robinson and Maxwell Hawkins must take the blame. They don't miss by much, but in this type play an inch is as much as a mile." The play closed in December, after 45 performances. That didn't stop the play's movie rights from selling "for some nice $ & ¢," according to the February '36 *WD*. However, no film resulted.

If Hawkins *had* been trying to make a go of freelancing, '36 may have been the year he threw in the towel. The play had hit a dead end, and his pulp output fell to three stories, a short to *Detective Fiction Weekly* (April 11), and two to *Dime Sports* (April, July). His daughter was born in '37, suggesting that he may have started a family at this time, with the resultant need for steady income.

The trail runs cold until the early years of WWII. Then, when the Navy was having difficulty attracting recruits to the submarine service, writers were given access to subs, sailors, and documents, and encouraged to glorify the cause. Hawkins was one of these. At the time a reporter for the International News Service, he spent six months at East Coast sub bases researching a book. The efforts of Hawkins, and three other writers, came to light when the Navy suppressed their work from publication, explaining only that the combined detail in the four books would reveal tactics and operations unknown to the enemy ("Silenced Submarines," *Time*, August 23, 1943). Hawkins, apparently, turned some of his research into a *Saturday Evening Post* article, probably the biggest magazine score of his career. The *Post* advertised "Rescue in the Night" (July 17, 1943) with this blurb:

Blood-tingling true account of an American sub crew's amazing victory over raging, shark-infested seas to rescue a stranded band of Australian brothers-in-arms. An epic of heroism against impossible odds—this vivid report of the crew's return again and again to a Jap-held island, will hold you thrilled to the last line.

It wasn't until May 31, 1945 that Secretary of the Navy Forrestal authorized the (now) six books for publication. Hawkins' *Torpedoes Away, Sir! Our Submarine Navy in the Pacific* was published by Henry Holt in 1946, his only book.

He would have been about 52 then. After that, it seems he settled down to his newspaper career. His pulp career, so far as we know, wrapped up with a short in *Fifteen Sports Stories* (May '49), and one last detective story in *Popular Detective* (May '50). He died, October 4, 1962, in Westport, Connecticut, where he had lived for three years. He was survived by his wife, both children, and his older brother.

ON NEXT MONTH'S CALENDAR

*Gripping, action=shot Detective
and Gangster Stories!*

The
CULT of the CORPSES

By Maxwell Hawkins

Into the dark depths of New York's underworld came a new horror! A sinister, gruesome band who kept the skulls of the gangsters they put on the spot! Terrible and ghastly was their charnel house—the storeroom of dreadful souvenirs! . . . . Benton McCray and Nan Collette made the mistake of discovering the existence of this heinous order! And the "Cult of the Corpses" meted out to transgressors the horrible fate of the "zombie"—the living dead!

*A new kind of a gangster story . . . . You've
never read anything like it before!*

-- Also --

William H.
Stueber

Joe
Archibald

Carl McK.
Saunders

Eugene A.
Clancy

Detective-Dragnet, December 1930

Cult of the Corpses

Into the dark depths of New York's underworld came a new horror! A sinister, gruesome band who kept the skulls of the gangsters they put on the spot! Terrible and ghastly was their charnel house—the storeroom of dreadful souvenirs! . . . Benton McCray and Nan Collette made the mistake of discovering the existence of this heinous order. And the Cult of the Corpses meted out to transgressors the horrible fate of the "zombie"—the living dead!

I

GREEN EYES

EARLY MORNING. THE BRIGHT LIGHTS IN THE GAYETY GROTTO, newest and most popular of Broadway night clubs, suddenly grew dim. Through the smoke-saturated atmosphere, the white shirt fronts of the men gleamed in ghostly vagueness, matched by the pale faces and shoulders of the women in

*McCray gripped the machete and
started toward the hooded monster.
He'd have to finish him fast!*

evening gowns. Except for a scattering of whispered comment, the babel of conversation, which had filled the large, low-ceilinged room, was hushed.

Benton McCray, former lieutenant in the United States Marine Corps, now connected with the district attorney's office, leaned across the table to his companion, a pretty girl in her early twenties, with waving copper-colored hair.

"Now we'll see the great Zareta, Nan. She's really quite the latest sensation."

Nan Collette turned her chair slightly so she could view the patch of polished dance floor better. A spotlight beam cut through the murk and into its white circle whirled a feminine figure, scantily draped.

There was a ripple of applause, quickly stilled. Zareta accepted it with a smile that displayed her glistening teeth. Then as the orchestra swung into a slow sensuous rhythm, she began her dance. It was a beautiful thing in its way, yet beneath its graceful movements was an almost macabre menace, accentuated by the panther-like suppleness of the swarthy long-eyed dancer.

"It's weird," Nan whispered with a faint shudder.

"Wait," McCray replied softly.

He apparently was watching the dancer intently, but actually it was through the medium of his ears that he was receiving his most startling sensation. The *largo* and oddly accented cadence of the music had awakened in him a vague sense of uneasiness.

Dimly McCray seemed to feel himself transported back fifteen years—to a black, jungle-tangled valley beneath a hot tropical sky, encrusted with stars. With a flash of unpleasant recollection he recognized the source of the wild quality of the music—the drummer was pounding the big bass drum, turned on its side, with the heel of his palm—in that instant it all came back to him, and as he passed his hand across his forehead, he could feel tiny beads of cold sweat.

Zareta glided from the spotlight, but a second later returned to the calcium glare. Now she was holding in her two hands, extended at length before her, a gruesome chalky object, on which she fastened her eyes with a mocking smile. A gasp, half of astonishment, half of horror, swept over the crowded room. Nan leaned toward McCray.

"Ghastly—though, of course, the thing isn't real."

McCray shook his head. "It's a human skull, all right," he murmured. "One of the Broadway columnists even has it that it's the skull of one of her dead lovers, a gangster who was put on the spot."

"She's Spanish, isn't she?" Nan asked.

"That's what they say. But there never was a dance like this thing danced in sunny Spain, if you ask me."

Abruptly the room was in total darkness. The music grew softer in an unearthly strain, almost funereal in its tempo, and through the blackness suddenly beamed twin shafts of green light. They came from the eye-sockets of the skull, which Zareta continued to hold in her hands, and she let them fall full upon her face as she swayed to the eerie music. In the green glow her features seemed covered with mold, like a creature of the other world that had crawled from a shallow grave.

Nan involuntarily groped for McCray's hand, and when she found it he could feel that her own was moist and cold.

The green eyes of the skull went out, A second later the orchestra broke into a lively foxtrot and the Grotto was flooded with brilliance. A nervous laugh of relief, followed by a salvo of applause, burst from the gathering at the tables. Several couples arose from their seats and presently the floor where Zareta had executed her bizarre act was packed with chattering patrons.

With an effort McCray threw off the uncanny spell the music had cast over him. In the full light, it seemed ridiculous that an almost dead memory could have been brought to his mind by the mere rhythmic beating of a drum. And yet—his eyes sought the drummer, an ivory-toothed and grinning negro, who was now busily tossing the sticks into the air and catching them. His face seemed familiar.

"It's positively repulsive, Ben!" Nan exclaimed.

"Yes, it really is, when you stop to think of it," he agreed. "But it's what the sensation seekers who frequent this place are after, I suppose."

Nan gave a little shrug. "That Zareta woman fills me with the creeps."

A tall man in immaculate evening attire got up from a table not far away and headed toward them, pausing now and then to speak to guests who were not dancing. His face was slightly flushed, and, although ostensibly there was no liquor sold in the Grotto, it was evident he had been drinking. But he was in perfect control of all his faculties.

"Good evening, Mr. McCray," he said, halting at Ben's table.

"Hello, Carter," the other replied. "How are you finding things tonight?"

"First rate," Carter said. "Zareta is proving a big drawing card. Quite a jolly little performance she puts on, isn't it?" he added with a little laugh.

"Jolly as a cemetery at midnight," McCray agreed dryly.

He presented the tall man to Nan, with a word of explanation.

"Mr. Carter is one of the proprietors of the Grotto."

Carter acknowledged the introduction with a polished bow. This man was engaged in a rather dubious sort of business, but it was clear he was not a graduate of the racketeer school of manners. There was a dignified ease and assurance about him.

"Did you enjoy Zareta's work, Miss Collette?"

"I can't say that I did," Nan confessed with engaging frankness.

"Well, at any rate she's unusual," Carter suggested. "And no one can deny that she's a talented dancer. Rather fascinating, too, in her dark way. Would you care to dance, perhaps?" he added.

Catching Ben's nod of assent, Nan stood up and Carter guided her through the dancing throng with the deftness born of long experience with jammed night club floors.

McCray settled back comfortably and surveyed the scene before him leisurely, but with an innate keenness of observation that permitted no detail to escape him. It was a motley crowd, a crowd that ranged from the highest to the lowest stratum of society.

Two men talking earnestly at one of the tables caught his attention. They were in dinner clothes, but neither seemed to Ben to be entirely comfortable in them. One of the men called his companion's notice to the dance floor just as Carter and Nan passed them, although McCray wasn't sure whether it was the man or the girl he was indicating. The second man glanced up quickly, then turned back with a negative shake of his head.

Carter was speaking earnestly to Nan. She seemed mildly interested in what he was saying, but observing Ben, she gave him an amused wink.

As the music came to a sudden stop with a wail of saxophones, McCray saw Zareta emerge from the dressing rooms behind the large shell, under which the colored orchestra sat. The dancer had changed her costume for a gown of Nile green, which set off every move of her seductive figure. What surprised him, however, was that on one side of the modish creation had been sewn an irregular patch of coarse red cloth, which extended up over the left side of her breast.

"She seems partial to green," Ben thought.

Zareta hesitated a moment, leaning languidly against the edge of the shell, while her glance roamed the room. Suddenly she stared, and Ben fancied a greenish tinge came into her large dark eyes, fringed with heavy curling lashes.

"A reflection from the green dress," he decided with an amused shrug. His nerves were playing him tricks. That barbaric dance with its weird music had gotten under his skin. But he continued to watch Zareta.

Following her gaze, he suddenly discovered with a start that the object of her fixed attention was Nan Collette.

Zareta, seeming to sense McCray's scrutiny, quickly veiled her eyes with her long lashes. Then she slipped into the crowd that was milling about the floor on the way back to the tables, and was lost to Ben's sight.

"Now, what the devil—" he muttered.

Carter and Nan approached. He was bending over her confidentially and speaking close to her ear in a low tone. On Nan's face was the same expression of amused tolerance McCray had noticed when the couple were dancing.

She sat down with a word of thanks to Carter. The man bowed, made a friendly wave toward Ben, and then returned to his own table, where he had been sitting alone.

"An amusing conversationalist, I take it," McCray ventured with a quizzical smile.

"It *was* funny," Nan replied. "He persisted in telling me how much I resembled some other girl—a girl he once was very much interested in. Said that's why he had sought a dance with me. Rather an old line for a man of his sophistication, but then he was a little bit—er—oiled, as they say."

"An odd chap," McCray mused.

"Who is he, anyway?" Nan asked.

Ben turned the question over in his mind for several seconds before answering.

"To a good many people he's the enigma of Broadway. I suppose I shouldn't have let you dance with him, but I wanted you to get all the thrill you could out of our little expedition."

"Is he actually as dangerous as all that?" she laughed.

"Not exactly dangerous, but his reputation's a bit unsavory. He appeared in these parts several years ago—from somewhere out west. Some say Chicago. Anyway, he seemed to have plenty of money and in a short time had chiseled into this night club racket."

McCray looked across the room and noticed that Zareta had joined the object of their conversation at his table. Her presence didn't appear to be very welcome to Carter, for he was scowling into his half-empty glass.

Zareta, however, was ignoring his unfriendliness and talking to him earnestly, leaning over the table from time to time to impress her words by pressing on his arm. She turned and shot a glance at Nan. Carter, too, looked up, but seeing that McCray was watching them, immediately lowered his eyes to his glass again. Then he shook his head in a firm negative, and a second later got up abruptly and stalked across the dance floor in the direction of the entrance.

Zareta sat for a time, her shoulders drooping. Then she also rose from the table and her steps took her once more to the dressing rooms behind the orchestra shell, from which she had made her appearance only a short while before.

Just before she vanished from sight, she turned and looked squarely at Nan, and again Ben imagined he saw in her eyes that uncanny greenish light. He glanced at Nan, but she seemed entirely unconscious of the dancer's interest in her and of the pantomime which he had just witnessed.

With a shouted "Hey! Hey! Folks!" the orchestra started another number. Nan decided she was too tired to dance and she and Ben sat watching the gyrations of the others. Finally she turned to him.

"I think, Ben, we'd better be leaving. It must be almost morning."

He looked at his watch. "Quarter of three."

McCray beckoned their waiter, paid the exorbitant check and they left the table, making their way with some difficulty past the dancing pack on the floor.

Just as they reached the door which led from the main room into a small foyer and the cloak room, a tall broad-shouldered man blocked their progress.

"Stop that music!" he shouted. His voice rang with authority above the din of the orchestra. The musicians turned frightened faces toward him and abruptly the big room grew deathly quiet.

"Sorry everybody," the newcomer said, lowering his voice, "but I'll have to ask you all to take your seats—and keep them, until I give the word."

"A raid," McCray whispered to Nan. Then he looked sharply at the man in the doorway. Behind him he noticed several policemen in uniform. "Wait here, Nan. I'll talk to this man."

"Hello, Spayne," Ben said, recognizing the big man as the lieutenant in charge of the detectives in the Times Square district. Spayne nodded in recognition.

"Good evening, Mr. McCray."

Ben lowered his voice. "I suppose it will be all right if I go on out and escort this young lady home. I guess you know where to reach me, and I'll vouch for her appearance if necessary. I may even have to handle the case," he added with a grin.

"Well," Spayne agreed, "I guess that'll be all O.K. But this is pretty serious business."

Ben was surprised at the grim look on the detective's face. It was not often that the men on the force took these raids so much to heart.

"Serious? What's wrong?"

Spayne dropped his voice to a whisper.

"They've just bumped off Carter! Turned a machine gun on him!" The detective's lips tightened ominously. "And that ain't all. While they was sprayin' the damn thing around, they got a fellow who was walking by and"—there was the semblance of a catch in his voice—"and the best pal I had on the force—Tom Illick!"

II

Burned Matches

It was almost noon before Benton McCray so much as fluttered an eyelid, which would have seemed out of place in an enterprising assistant district attorney on any other day. But this was Sunday. Besides, when one has greeted the dawn on his way home, after an eventful experience at a night club, the pillow feels pretty good.

And when McCray did awake it wasn't with fluttering eyelids, but bolt upright in the bed in his bachelor apartment, acutely aware that someone was ringing his door bell violently.

He slipped his feet into bedroom slippers and grabbed a bathrobe from a nearby chair. Crossing rapidly to the foyer, he threw open the door into the hallway. Lieutenant Spayne was standing outside.

"Sorry to bother you," the detective said apologetically, "but I'm trying to work fast on the killings last night, and there's some information maybe you can give me. You remember about last night—or rather this morning—don't you?"

"Certainly," McCray said. "Come in!"

Spayne stepped into the apartment and accepted the chair which Ben drew forward for him. He looked curiously about the comfortably furnished quarters and then at McCray, who had dropped into another chair and was waiting patiently for Spayne to state his business. The detective cleared his throat apologetically.

"It's about the young lady who was with you last night," he began.

Ben stiffened. "What about her?" he snapped.

"Now don't get excited, Mr. McCray," cautioned Spayne. "All I want to do is ask her a few questions—don't forget that when I let you take her out of the Grotto after the shooting, you said you'd produce her if she was wanted."

"So I did," Ben agreed more calmly. "But see here, Spayne, I don't want to get Miss Collette mixed up in this affair. You know yourself it's just another gang fight."

"Well, I'm not saying it ain't," agreed the detective, "but—"

"Furthermore," interrupted Ben, "I can't see the need of having the name of a perfectly respectable girl dragged into the papers in such a connection."

"That's just why I came to see you so soon," Spayne said.

"What do you want to question her about?"

"Here's the situation, Mr. McCray," the detective said. "About five minutes before I showed up in the Grotto, this guy Carter come down the stairs. He was alone and started up the street to where his car was parked, see?"

"Sure."

"But he never reached it. Three gorillas in a black sedan came down the street. According to the door man, one of 'em shouts, 'Give it to him!' With that they opens up with a Thompson sub-machine gun, I imagine it was, and Carter drops. Hit eight times! But they don't shut her off. Just keep the old organ grinding away, and then's when the passerby, a fellow named Pringle from Bellmore, gets his. Illick comes up on the double quick and one of the bullets drills him right through the heart.

"I guess they decided they'd done enough harm for one time, and, so the doorman says, they stepped on the gas and disappeared around the corner onto Sixth Avenue."

"Where'd you come into it?" asked McCray.

"I was a couple of blocks down on Broadway, when I heard that machine gun to stutter. You couldn't fool me on the sound. I'd heard it too often in France.

"I hot-footed it up as fast as I could, but when I got there, the three of 'em—Carter, Pringle and Illick, was all stretched out dead. A couple of harness bulls had beat me to it, and a couple more arrived just after I got there. I put one of 'em on guard over the entrance. Then I went on up to the Grotto. Get me?"

"Check," Ben said. "Go on!"

"After you left, we got all the names—some pretty important ones, too, if you ask me," Spayne added with a squint. "We let all the guests go then, but the ones who worked there—the orchestra, entertainers, waiters and Mink Magnozzi—we hauled over to the station for questioning."

"Who's Mink Magnozzi?" McCray asked.

"I thought you knew him. He's Carter's partner in the joint. As near as I can make out, Carter put up the dough and furnished the ideas. Magnozzi was the guy who knew how to run a night club and had the connections."

"I place him now," McCray nodded. "The smooth little wop who used to stand near the entrance and look the patrons over. What did you learn at the station?"

Spayne scowled. "Not much. It was the same old story. They all claimed they didn't know a damn thing about it. Magnozzi swore he'd had no difficulties with Carter and that they weren't in any jam with the liquor mobs." He paused. "The only thing in the way of a clew, we got from the Spanish dame."

"Zareta—the dancer?"

"That's her."

McCray found himself leaning forward attentively. Swiftly there passed through his mind an image of the exotic entertainer as he had last glimpsed her—the green eyes!

"What did you get out of her?"

"That," said the detective quietly, "is where the young lady you were with comes in."

Ben's manner became impatient. "Spill it!" he demanded brusquely. "Don't be so damn mysterious!"

For answer, Spayne reached into his pocket and brought forth a crumpled piece of brown paper, such as is used in stores to wrap up parcels, and handed it to McCray.

"This Zareta had only been working at the Grotto for a couple of weeks," the detective said, by way of comment. "At first she and Carter were kind of sweet on each other, but it didn't last long. Either she cooled off or he did. I kind of think he was the one."

Ben, however, was paying only slight attention to Spayne's words. His eyes were glued on the irregular scrap of paper. Not without some difficulty was he able to read the writing; its characters, made with a blunt black pencil, were poorly formed, almost childish:

Watch for red head if c leaves with her lay off if he goes alone give him the works

That was all. There was no salutation, no signature. McCray turned the paper over curiously, but the reverse side was blank. He handed it back to

Spayne, who put it carefully back in his pocket.

"Well?" Ben's tone bore a hint of sarcasm.

"It's just this way, Mr. McCray," Spayne said doggedly. "You're connected with the D.A.'s office, and I know you're on the up and up. So's the girl, so far as I know. But I've gotta run down every tip, haven't I—that's my business, ain't it?"

"Of course," Ben agreed.

"The girl you was with had red hair?"

"Yes."

"And the headwaiter said Carter danced with her—not more'n ten minutes before he was bumped off."

"Yes, that's right—"

"Well, then I gotta question her. He may have said something that would help us. I understand he was talking pretty earnestly to her."

Ben lighted a cigarette, while he was thinking over Spayne's words.

"All right," he said at last. "I can see your point of view—and it's sound. But remember—the newspaper boys don't get a word of this!"

"I tell them what they ought to know, and that's all," the detective said significantly.

"Listen to me, before we start." McCray spoke crisply. "Miss Collette has been a friend of mine for three years. She comes from a respectable family up in Rochester and holds a very responsible position as head of the women's department for a Wall Street bond house. She'd never been to the Grotto in her life until last night. We went to a theatre and then up there to dance, because she said she wanted to see a lively night club in full swing. Do you understand?"

"Why, sure, Mr. McCray," Spayne agreed.

"I introduced her to Carter. She danced with him; then came right back to our table. But here's the important thing from my point of view. It's not generally known. Miss Collette and I are engaged to be married. Now you can appreciate why I don't want her name connected with a slimy gang murder!"

"Mr. McCray," the detective said earnestly, "I'll see that there's no publicity, but—"

"Oh, I realize you have to question her. I'll telephone her to expect us, and then slip into some clothes."

He disappeared into the other room, returning a few minutes later and nodding to Spayne.

"She says it will be all right to come right over. Make yourself comfortable while I dress."

Five minutes later McCray was ready. He led the way to the foyer and opened the door for Spayne. As he turned to close the door behind him, his eyes dropped to the floor. The detective had already started toward the stairway, so missed McCray's gasp of surprise—almost horror. Ben stood motionless for a couple of seconds. Then he stooped over with a nervous laugh.

Lying on the hall floor at his door sill was a tiny cross formed of two burned matches tightly bound with red twine.

He slipped the strange object into his pocket and joined Spayne. His manner was calm, but inwardly Ben had a feeling of uneasiness, which he could account for, but which his common sense told him was too fantastic to give serious consideration.

III

IN NAN'S APARTMENT

ON THEIR WAY OVER TO NAN COLLETTE'S APARTMENT, Spayne explained to McCray how Zareta had come into possession of the cryptic note—or at least how she said she had.

"This Spanish dame," the detective said, as they settled back in their seat in the taxi, "says she's just about to begin her dance when she sees the paper on the floor. She picks it up, so she won't be kicking it around while she's dancing. Then she notices there's some writing on it, and being curious like all women, sticks it in her dress."

"She didn't have much in the way of a dress on," remarked Ben dryly.

"Well," she managed to hang onto it somehow until she got back to the dressing room, according to her story," Spayne replied. "Then she read it and a few minutes later comes out and sees Carter dancing with a redheaded girl. The thing looks plain to her. The 'c' in the note is Carter; the redhead is Miss Collette.

"Zareta claims she took Carter aside and tried to warn him. But he just got sore, and told her she was crazy. That's her story, and that's why I've gotta talk to Miss Collette."

McCray was silent, recalling to his mind the scene of the night club. Spayne's account was borne out in part by what Ben recalled. It explained the earnest conversation Zareta had had with Carter, following the dance with Nan, when the dancer was sitting at his table. It explained, too, his air of scowling displeasure and abrupt departure from the table and the room—to his death!

They drew up before a tall apartment building on West Seventy-Second Street, a scant half-block from Riverside Drive.

The colored elevator operator stopped the cage at the eleventh floor. Both men got out and Ben led the way down the hall. Neither observed that the operator did not start down again immediately, but if they had, would probably not have attached any particular significance to his delay at the moment.

The building was filled with small apartments, ranging in size from one to three rooms. At one of the numerous doors on the floor, McCray halted. He pressed the small white button of the electric bell and waited.

There was no response and again Ben pushed his finger on the button, this time holding it for a considerable time. Faintly they could hear it ringing within the apartment, but still no one came to their summons.

"That's strange," Ben muttered. "When I talked to her on the phone, I said we'd be right over and she said she'd be waiting here for us."

"Maybe she's just stepped out and will be right back," Spayne suggested. "That taxi brought us here in pretty good time."

With a faint feeling of worry, Ben tried the bell for the third time, and when it brought no answer, he started back toward the elevator.

"We might as well wait downstairs in the lounge—and meet her when she comes in. There are chairs down there," he said.

On the way down in the elevator, Ben spoke to the operator. "Do you know Miss Collette when you see her?" he asked.

"Yes, sir," the man replied. "She lives in 11-B." His voice was quiet, but Ben noticed it bore no trace of the southern negro accent. From the West Indies, McCray realized. Or a native of the north.

"Have you seen her go out?"

The car had reached the main floor and the colored operator waited until he had pulled open the doors, before replying. Even then there seemed to be some hesitancy on his part, as though he were trying to recall.

"Yes, sir," he said finally. "I remember she went out just about five or ten minutes ago. I ain't seen her come back."

Ben felt a sensation of relief. Nan had undoubtedly gone out on some errand and would return shortly. He offered Spayne a cigar as the two men took chairs in the rather elaborate lobby, from where they had a clear view of the entrance to the building, Absently he picked up the first section of a Sunday paper, which was lying on the table beside him. He glanced casually over the front page and then turned it over. Suddenly he leaned forward intently and gave a little gasp.

"My God!"

His eyes, a look of panic in them, were glued to the paper as he read. Then he laughed, hollowly, nervously.

He handed the paper to Spayne, pointing to a picture at the top of the second column. The detective lieutenant, his curiosity whetted by McCray's actions, looked at it carefully.

He saw a picture of a more than ordinarily pretty woman, her hair curling delicately around her forehead. But the dull lifeless expression on the face, in spite of extensive retouching by the artist, would have told an experienced newspaper man that the photographer had not hesitated to venture into the morgue to get his "shot."

Above was the caption:

FIRE TRUCK VICTIM!

Spayne, after scrutinizing the picture, dropped his eyes to the printed matter beneath, which told the story.

> An unidentified woman was struck and instantly killed shortly before one o'clock this morning by the truck of Engine Company 43 as she was crossing Thirty-sixth Street at Seventh Avenue.
> According to the fireman and driver, the woman stepped from a taxi parked at the curb directly into the path of the speeding fire truck, responding to a false alarm on Ninth Avenue. Nick Pantagres, 33, of 662 York Avenue, the cabman, is being questioned by the police.
> The woman was about thirty years old, five-feet two-inches tall, and weighed about 120 pounds. She has red hair and blue eyes and was wearing a gray ensemble of expensive quality, but the maker's label had been removed from the garment. No means of identification were found on the body, which is at the City Morgue.

"Well?" Spayne lifted a questioning eyebrow.

"It gave me quite a start, until I read the story and saw what time the accident occurred," McCray said.

"How's that?"

"Oh, I forgot for the minute that you had never met Miss Collette. That picture in the paper is a perfect likeness of her," Ben explained.

The detective became thoughtful. Then he looked again at the picture and account of the accident.

"Funny," he remarked. "It says here the dead woman had red hair, too."

"Coincidence," Ben said, dismissing the matter.

"Sure, but"—Spayne tore the page of the paper, removing the part containing the picture and story of the fire truck accident, and placed it in his pocket—"you never can tell."

McCray took out his watch and glanced at it; then he got to his feet quickly.

"I wonder what's keeping her," he muttered. "We've been waiting here almost twenty minutes." For a short time he paced back and forth and then turned to Spayne. "I'm not entirely easy about this situation," Ben confessed.

"Think I'll try that telephone, just for luck."

He entered the public telephone booth in one corner of the lobby. Presently he emerged, a worried expression on his face.

"Operator reports the line out of order," he said to Spayne.

The detective looked up from the paper he was reading. "Well, they do get out of kilter now and then, you know," he suggested in an effort to quiet the fear, which was becoming more and more apparent in Ben.

"But, man, I talked to her only a little while ago. It was all right then."

He walked across the lobby to the elevator, where the colored operator was leaning against the opened door, waiting for any passengers who might come in. Ben spoke to him briskly.

"Sure you didn't make any mistake about seeing Miss Collette leave here?"

The negro shook his head. "No, sir. She went out."

"Alone?"

The operator considered. "I don't exactly remember whether she was alone or not—" he hesitated, but as McCray's eyes bored into him, he stammered on. "Come to think of it, there—there was another lady with her, maybe."

Ben returned to where Spayne was sitting. "Listen," he said, lowering his voice, "there's something wrong here. I've a hunch that elevator man is lying to me."

"What do you want to do?" the detective asked.

"I'm going to investigate Miss Collette's apartment! Come on!"

He walked rapidly back toward the elevator man; Spayne followed close behind him.

"Where's the superintendent of this building?" Ben snapped.

"What you want him for?" The operator's tone was far from servile.

"I want the passkey so I can get into Miss Collette's apartment," Ben answered grimly.

"No, sir, you can't see the superintendent. Today's Sunday and I ain't going to disturb him," the colored man said, almost belligerently.

Spayne reached out a large hand and seized the fellow by the neck of his tight-fitting blouse with a grip that made his eyes bulge in their black sockets.

"Is—that—so!" the detective barked. He turned back his coat with his free hand so his badge could be seen, and twisted the frightened negro about. "Take a look at that! Now you and I are going to the superintendent right away! Get me?"

He released his hold. The elevator operator gulped once or twice, found his breath. "Yes, sir! Yes, sir!" he blurted out, thoroughly cowed by the angry expression on Spayne's face. "Come right this way, Mister Officer."

McCray waited at the elevator, while the detective and his guide disappeared through a door leading off the rear of the lobby. His feeling of alarm was growing more and more definite; some sixth sense seemed to warn him of disaster.

Spayne and the elevator man presently reappeared in the lobby. They were accompanied by a short, heavy-set individual in shirt sleeves, who carried a large ring with numerous keys on it.

"This is Mr. Manning, the superintendent," Spayne said to McCray. "He says he's got a key that'll do the trick."

As the three of them approached the door to Apartment 11-B, Manning fumbled with the keys on the ring.

"I'm not sure whether I ought to do this, gentlemen," he said in a mild sort of protest.

"Forget it!" growled Spayne. "You know who I am, and Mr. McCray here is not only a friend of the young lady who lives here, but he's also an assistant district attorney."

Manning at last found the proper key and, slipping the lock back, swung the door wide open.

Ben strode into the apartment with a quick and anxious step. Spayne followed, but Manning, still not entirely satisfied as to the propriety of what he had done, remained near the door.

"Nan!" McCray called. And again, "Nan!"

There was no answer. Spayne behind him, he walked into the small living room. Everything was in perfect order. Through the two partially opened windows, with their attractive chintz curtains, a cool breeze was blowing up from the bay, eight miles south.

In the sink of the tiny kitchenette were a few dirty dishes, which to Ben, knowing Nan's passion for neatness and order, indicated that she had just finished her breakfast when interrupted.

A glance in the large closet off the entry hall revealed nothing but clothing. He opened the door to the bathroom. The place was empty. Then the two men turned to the closed door at the far end of the hall, which led to the only other room in the apartment, the bedroom.

Ben placed his hand on the knob; he was half afraid to turn it, dreading what he might find on the other side of the portal. Then with a tightening of his jaw muscles, he swung it wide and stepped in.

A second later he uttered a low cry of alarm.

IV

A STRANGE CLEW

THE BEDROOM WAS EMPTY, but, in contrast to the rest of the apartment, the furnishings were in wild disorder, signs of a terrific struggle. Two small rugs on the polished floor were pushed into irregular heaps, a chair was overturned, and alongside it lay the little telephone table. The telephone itself was in a corner across the room, its cord torn violently from the bell box.

Ben felt as though an icy hand were clutching his heart.

"Come in and shut that door behind you!" Spayne's voice snapped out in sharp command to Manning. The superintendent stepped into the foyer, his eyes wide, and quickly closed the door leading to the outer hall. The detective turned to McCray.

"This looks damn bad," he muttered. "You're sure you talked to her over the phone—it couldn't have been some other woman's voice you heard?"

Ben shook his head. "No, I'd recognize Nan's voice in a million," he said.

"Then one of two things has happened here in the last hour," Spayne declared. "Either Miss Collette was overpowered and carried away alive or—" The detective had no desire to torture McCray, but years in police work had made him callous and he knew there was little to be gained by beating about the bush. "Or else she's been killed, and her murderer—or murderers have removed the body!" he snapped.

Ben blanched, but took a firm hold of himself. "Well," he said, a dangerous quietness in his voice, "let's look the place over carefully, first of all."

Spayne began a minute search of the room for any clew to the mysterious attackers that might have been left behind.

McCray walked over to the large window, which, like the two in the living room, was partially opened and faced the south. The apartment was in the back of the building and looked toward the lower part of Manhattan. It was high up, and consequently there were no screens. Ben leaned out.

Below he saw a small courtyard, but it was bare. For one terrible second the thought had occurred to him that if Nan had been killed, her slayers might have hurled her body from the window. It would have been a way to have given the appearance of suicide, he realized, for almost daily the papers carried some account of a mangled human form being found below the windows of the towering buildings.

Then he noticed running along the side of the rear wall an ornamental ledge, about eight inches wide. It would have been a relatively simple matter for an iron nerved man to have made his way along it and gained access to the apartment Nan occupied. He walked across the room to where Manning was standing, his knees trembling with fright.

"Who lives in the adjoining apartments?"

Manning knit his brow. "A Mr. and Mrs. Wilson are in 11-C," he said. "That's the one nearer the elevator. The one on the other side, 11-A, is vacant."

"Have you a key?" Ben asked.

"We don't lock the empties, sir," Manning replied. "That's so the elevator man can show them to any prospective tenants that might come here."

McCray looked meaningly at Spayne, who had joined them.

"We'll take a look at 11-A first," he said and the detective nodded agreement. They left the apartment, Manning following timidly.

As they halted in front of 11-A, Spayne felt of a reassuring bulge on his hip. He saw Ben notice the gesture.

"Probably no need for it," the detective murmured, "but just in case there is, I like to know it'll slip out easy."

McCray laid his hand on the door knob. It yielded readily and they entered. The apartment they were in was a duplicate of the one they had left, but was completely unfurnished, although clean and newly decorated.

"Do you leave the windows up in your vacant apartments?" Ben asked Manning, pointing to one of the two windows in the living room.

The superintendent looked surprised. "No, we don't. The operators have orders to see that they're always closed after a prospect has looked at an apartment. In case of a sudden rain."

Ben strode to the open window. He examined the frame. Then his eyes narrowed.

"What do you make of that, Spayne?"

The detective followed the direction of his finger. On the recently painted white sill could be plainly seen the faint impression of a rubber heel. He whistled softly.

"Someone used this window as a door," he said, after a brief examination. "See, the soot on the outer sill is all scuffed about."

"That explains how they got into Nan's place beyond a doubt," McCray said. "Climbed out this window and then made their way along the ledge to her bedroom window."

Both men began a careful scrutiny of the other window frames and also the apartment itself. But their search revealed no other trace, not so much as a fingerprint.

"How about the Wilsons?" Ben asked the superintendent.

"I'm sure they're away," the man answered. "They spend their weekends at the shore during the nice weather."

"We'll look over their place," Ben said crisply.

Manning hesitated. "Well, gentlemen, I don't like—"

"You heard what Mr. McCray said," Spayne snapped, a hard glint in his eye. "We'll look over the Wilson apartment."

Without further protest, Manning led the way to 11-C and unlocked the door, after an insistent ringing on the bell had failed to evoke any response.

But there was nothing in there to help them. The windows were all closed and locked. Apparently there had been no one in the place since the owners left. Ben drew Spayne aside.

"I've a hunch that black elevator man knows a lot about this," he said in a low voice. "We'll go down and let you put a little pressure on him, if necessary."

As the three men walked toward the elevator, Ben questioned the superintendent. "Any other way to get up here besides the elevator? Any freight elevator in back?"

Manning shook his head. "There's just the one elevator in front, and, of course, the front stairs. It's one of the things that's bad about the design of the building."

They rang the elevator button. The indicator above the door, which showed what floor the car was on, pointed to "1" and failed to move, in spite of persistent ringing.

"Come on!" McCray exclaimed suddenly. "We're going down the stairs—fast!"

He ran toward the door which led to the stairway. Spayne, quick to grasp the situation, was close behind him, and Manning after a bewildered pause, followed. Ben, younger and in perfect physical trim, was the first to reach the lobby. Spayne arrived to find him standing before the open door of the elevator cage, a scowl of chagrin covering his brow.

"We're a couple of fools!" McCray snapped. "While we were gassing around up there, that black devil has ducked!"

Manning, breathless and worried, approached them.

"What's wrong?"

"Your elevator man has left you—and I don't believe he'll be back," McCray said dryly.

"What?" the superintendent gasped.

"He's mixed up in the disappearance of Miss Collette," Ben went on. He took a firm hold of Manning's coat lapel. "Your cue is to keep your mouth shut tight about all this. Get me?"

The superintendent, his face white, nodded. "Yes—yes, sir!"

"What's that elevator man's name and where does he live?"

"Why—why the only name I know for him is Louis," Manning stammered. "And I don't know where he lives."

"Don't you take the addresses of your help?" McCray demanded incredulously.

"Usually. But Louis had been here only a few days. I took him on the say-so of the colored operator who was here before him. I was just trying him out."

"You know where the fellow who recommended Louis lives?"

"Yes, sir. His name's Bruno Le Roy, lives at One Hundred and Thirty-fifth and Lexington, up in Harlem. He was a good man. I hated to lose him, but he got a better job playing in a dance orchestra."

Spayne, who had been standing deep in thought during the conversation between McCray and Manning, suddenly broke in.

"Got any kind of a rest room or locker room for the help?" he asked.

Manning nodded. "Yes, sir. A little room in the basement. Come this way."

They followed the superintendent down a flight of stairs and past the boiler room of the building. At a door, Manning paused.

"This is it, sir."

They entered the low-ceilinged room. On one side were half a dozen lockers.

"Which one did Louis use?" Spayne asked.

Manning pointed to a locker on the end, the door of which was standing ajar. The detective swung it wide and peered in. But even in the dim light of the one bulb hanging from the ceiling it was plain there was little or nothing in it.

"He took time to get his possessions. You make the elevator men leave their uniform coats here, don't you?" Spayne asked, pulling from the bottom of the compartment a crumpled uniform blouse.

"They wear their own clothes home," Manning said. "The uniforms belong to the building."

Spayne was down on one knee searching with his hands inside the locker. "That seems to be about all. No, wait a minute!" He stood up and walked to the light, better to examine the object which he was holding in his hand.

It was a small bag of some kind of leather, about two inches long and shaped like a miniature ham. From the top protruded several brightly colored feathers.

"Hell!" Spayne's tone was one of annoyance. "It's only a sort of a doll."

McCray, however, was staring at the odd object as though he had just seen a ghost. "My God!" The words came slowly, softly through his white lips. He took the feathered bag from Spayne and held it close to the light. The detective noticed that his hand trembled.

"No!" McCray whipped out the word almost desperately. "It's not a doll, Spayne! I wish to God that it were! It's—it's—" He paused, shuddering involuntarily, dreading to speak. "It's a voodoo hate-*ouanga!*"

V

BEN EXPLAINS

THE BUILDING WHERE MCCRAY'S QUARTERS WERE SITUATED had been at one time a city residence. It was of the familiar brownstone front style, now, however, remodeled into small bachelor apartments. The assistant district attorney occupied three rooms on the top floor at the front.

As soon as they had found chairs, Ben turned to the detective with a request to see the "doll" Spayne had dug out of the locker. From his pocket he pulled a penknife and cut a slit down the side of the little leather pouch. Then he carefully poured from it onto the table one of the queerest collection of items Spayne had even seen.

"I can't identify some of these things," Ben said, "but I recognize a few. These"—pointing with the blade of his knife—"are broken snake bones and those two larger pieces of bone are the jaws of a lizard. There are some black hen feathers here and also some black lamb's wool. I'd be willing to guess that the rest of the junk consists largely of sulphur grains, mud, salt, alum and a generous sprinkling of vegetable poisons."

Spayne was staring at the table with open-mouthed amazement. "What did you say this thing was?"

"A voodoo hate-*ouanga*." McCray was visibly agitated. "Of course, when I first looked at it I couldn't be sure whether it might not be a love-*ouanga*, or possibly the most common of all—a protective-*ouanga*. I really just guessed, until now, when I had a chance to see what was in it."

"Well, I'll be—" the detective began, but Ben interrupted him.

"Your voodoo worshipper wears one of these things around his neck almost all the time. *Ouango* is the Haitian name for a charm. There are charms to accomplish almost any desired result—cure illness, awaken affection, protect the wearer against evil, or to bring disaster and death to his enemies."

"How do you happen to know about these things?" Spayne asked in surprise.

"Simple," McCray replied. "I was, at one time, a second looey in the Marines. Went into Haiti in 1915. That's when President Guillaume Sam was assassinated—or rather butchered, because the enraged people of Port-au-Prince literally tore him limb from limb.

"I spent six months back in the hills surrounding the Cul-de-Sac plain chasing *cacos*, as they call the native bandits. It was then I got the inside dope on voodooism—largely from a native colored scout. But one night—"

Ben paused as though loath to recount what he had seen, with the thought of Nan's peril in his mind.

"Well, I was out reconnoitering alone. I came to the edge of a deep gully and on the far side I noticed an unusually bright campfire, as I thought.

"Through my field glasses, however, I was able to see that it was a ceremonial fire. Suddenly there came, almost like a beat of doom, the sound of drums—the *rada*-drums they are called. Many figures began to gather around the fire in front of a crude altar. I could recognize the *papaloi* and *mamaloi*, the voodoo priest and priestess.

"For an hour I watched through the glasses, actually only a few hundred yards away as the crow flies, but miles away because of the gorge in front of me. And at the finish—"

McCray passed his hands across his forehead and over his eyes.

"At the finish they made a human sacrifice!"

"My God, they killed a man?" Spayne exclaimed.

"A young girl," Ben answered softly. Then he spoke, and there was a brittle and determined quality in his voice. "That's the kind of thing we're up against, Spayne!"

"You mean—you—" the detective stammered, unable to grasp at once the full horror of the picture McCray was hinting at.

"I mean that somewhere in this city—probably in Harlem—there is an organization of voodoo worshippers, or worse still one of the fanatical offshoots of the religion, whose rites defy description in their stark horror and gruesomeness!"

"And you think Miss Collette—" Spayne hesitated to put his thought into words, but Ben understood and nodded.

"Probably the most ghastly of all the branches of voodooism," he said, "is the *culte des mortes*. It means the cult of the corpses. The members are the necromancers, the dealers in black magic, and in their ritual, disinterred bodies, or bodies of freshly slaughtered victims, play an essential part.

"God!" he exclaimed, his face twitching with fierce emotion. "If I thought Nan were in the power of the *culte des mortes*, I'd drop on my knees and pray that she be dead."

He sank into his chair and buried his head in his hands. Spayne was silent, his imagination conjuring up a spectacle too terrible to be expressed.

"The cult of the corpses," Ben said at last, when he had recovered his self-possession, "are said to control the *zombies*. Another Haitian Creole word. The natives believe that when the members of this cult can unearth a freshly buried body, they can recall it to a semblance of life, able to work and obey commands, but unable to talk or think, a helpless slave.

"These *zombies* have been pointed out to me. Personally, I thought them merely ordinary idiots and halfwits until a friend of mine, a Haitian doctor of highest intelligence and credibility, explained the thing to me.

"Although not subject to proof, it was his belief that the members of the *culte des mortes* administered a potent drug to perfectly well persons. This induced a coma, hardly distinguishable from death. After the burial, if the drugged victims were disinterred in time, they could be revived. But only partially so, for the drug destroyed a large portion of the brain cells and left the unfortunate soul, neither wholly dead nor wholly alive, without the slightest will power."

"Sort of like a bad dope addict," the detective suggested.

"Worse—a thousand times worse!" Ben exclaimed. "Now do you wonder," he added fiercely, "that I say I would rather see Miss Collette dead than in the hands of such black fiends?"

"By God!" Spayne muttered, jumping to his feet. "We'd better be getting on the trail. This thing"—pointing to the disemboweled hate-*ouanga*—"seems to mean pretty clearly that there's some of these voodoo worshippers mixed up in Miss Collette's disappearance."

"Just a minute!" McCray exclaimed. "This hate-*ouanga* by itself does not necessarily mean that. In order to make these charms most effective, according to the belief of the voodoo worshippers, they must be planted either on the person of the one against whom they are directed, or else in their living quarters."

"Well?" Spayne asked.

"Don't you see? This elevator man—this Louis, had this with him, waiting a chance to plant it in Miss Collette's apartment, but we came along and upset his plans."

"What makes you decide that?"

"As a matter of fact, the *ouanga* might have been directed against someone else. The fellow might have been carrying it around so the charm would operate against some personal enemy—except that I, too, received a voodoo warning!"

"What?" The detective seemed amazed at this sudden turn.

Ben nodded and drew from his pocket the crossed burned matches, bound with red twine, which he had picked up from in front of his door as he and Spayne left the apartment earlier. He laid it beside the remains of the hate-*ouanga* on the table, explaining to the detective where he had found it.

"It's a voodoo warning. It startled me when I first saw it. Then I dismissed it as just coincidence. Some little kid's handiwork," he said. "But now, I can see that it was placed there by one of the black devils with some mysterious incantation designed to keep me from interfering with the execution of their sinister schemes!"

Ben's manner became dangerously calm as he spoke.

"Here is our plan of action," he said. "First you and I will head for Harlem and try to locate the negro Bruno Le Roy, the one Manning mentioned, and through him try to get on the trail of Louis."

"And if we can't find either of them?" Spayne asked, yielding to Ben's leadership without realizing it.

"In that event," McCray replied grimly, "we go right to the Gayety Grotto, because—" He broke off abruptly and lifted a warning finger to his lips. His eyes turned toward the door that opened to the outside hallway, and then he glanced at the open transom above it.

On tiptoe, he made his way noiselessly to the foyer, where he halted for a second. Spayne, every muscle tense, watched him with hawk-like intensity.

Slowly McCray's hand moved out until it reached the door knob and closed around it. Then with a swift motion he flung the door open. There was a sound of running feet as Ben leaped through the doorway in pursuit. Spayne jumped to his feet and started after him; his speed doubled at a choking call for help.

VI

WHAT HAPPENED TO NAN?

WHEN BENTON MCCRAY TELEPHONED NAN COLLETTE that he and Spayne were on their way over to her apartment, she was in the midst of a late and leisurely breakfast. Somewhat surprised at the mid-day visit, for Ben had not explained the purpose of their call, she hurried through with the meal and then carried the soiled dishes to the sink, making a mental note to wash them later.

Although she had had less than her usual quota of sleep, Nan appeared bright-eyed and fresh, her clear cool skin seeming to glow in harmony with the cream negligee she was wearing.

"I wonder what's the proper costume for receiving a lieutenant of detectives," she said to herself, and then laughed out loud. "I suppose something in stripes would be *de rigueur*."

She crossed the little hallway, her mules making a joyful patter on the hardwood floor. Unsuspecting, she pushed the bedroom door open and stepped into the room, closing the door behind her. As she turned, her eyes grew wide with terror.

Nan opened her mouth to scream, but the sound was choked back into her throat by a huge black hand that closed over her mouth. An arm, with muscles like bands of steel, was flung around her. Nan was not a large girl, but many hours spent on tennis courts and the golf links in her schoolgirl days had given her a supple and strong body. Added to this, fright gave her strength, and she fought for her life.

With a desperate effort she wriggled from the encircling arm, but the black hand still kept all but a few faint sounds from issuing from her mouth.

She lunged toward the telephone and just as her hand closed upon it, the burly negro's arm shot around her again and she was dragged backward, the instrument in her hand yanked from the wall.

Frantically the terrified girl strove to free herself from the savage clutch of her enemy, but the effort was futile. In a few minutes she was exhausted. Suddenly she heard him speak, and realized that a second person had entered the room, whom she was unable to see.

"Now!"

Nan felt a stinging sensation in her arm. Immediately she sensed herself grow weak, unable to move even her eyelids without a great effort. The room seemed filled with gray haze, through which the familiar objects assumed weird form. Then everything dissolved into a black void.

When Nan awoke, it was with a heavy sense of foreboding and alarm depressing her mind, and a sharp pain shooting through the muscles of her body.

She opened her eyes. Where was she? The room was in complete darkness and for an instant the thought flitted through her mind that she was dead and this was her tomb.

Then little by little, like fragments of a vaguely remembered nightmare, her hazy impressions of the events following her capture were pieced together in her consciousness. The drug had almost worn off, but her mind was still in a confused state. What was the meaning of all this?

Suddenly stark, hideous terror gripped her. She thought of Ben and tried to call his name, but her vocal cords refused to respond. Only a faint hiss came from between her parched lips. Then she heard a door open and immediately afterwards the room was filled with light which blinded her for a second.

She looked up, and as her eyes gradually became accustomed to the illumination, Nan could feel her blood turning cold. A sinuous long-eyed woman was moving slowly into the room, her lips curled back from her white teeth in a leer of cruel triumph.

Again Nan tried to call out, and again she was unable to utter more than a weak hissing noise. The visitor, however, read the question in her expression.

"Ah, you recognize me! Yes, it is Zareta!"

She halted by the cot on which Nan was now sitting upright. For a moment she remained motionless, gloating over the other woman's helplessness.

A burst of wild rage possessed Nan. She sprang from the cot, heedless of the agony the effort brought to her aching limbs, and faced Zareta.

The dancer seemed to delight in the suffering Nan was undergoing, but otherwise appeared unmoved. It was clear that she had no fear of Nan's wrath.

"I know—I know. You would like to kill me," Zareta sneered. "But it would do you no good to try, my dear. Before you could lay a finger upon me—" She glanced around the room, with a significant shrug of those expressive shoulders which had fascinated the habitués of the Grotto.

"Here, drink this!" Zareta exclaimed suddenly, and Nan noticed for the first time that she was carrying in one hand a tall glass containing an amber liquid. She extended it toward Nan, who hesitated.

"Don't be afraid," Zareta said with an unpleasant laugh. "It isn't poison. I have not gone to all the trouble of having you brought to me just to kill you—yet!" She stressed the final word, with faint arching of her narrow delicately molded brows. Then she suddenly became brisk, almost snarling.

"Don't be a little fool. It's an antidote that will relieve you of the aftereffects of the drug and cure the paralysis of your vocal cords."

Nan took the glass and raised it to her lips. The liquid felt cool and slightly sweetish on her tongue. With a quick movement she drained the glass. Almost immediately the pain seemed to leave her body; her head, too, began to clear.

"Let me warn you that resistance is useless," Zareta said. "Now, since you're feeling better, we'll go. I was a little afraid those helpers of mine might have drugged you too heavily. They're overenthusiastic in my cause at times. If they had, it would have been a shame, my dear, because I have need of you. Let us go! You first!"

VII

THE LIVING DEAD

FOLLOWING DIRECTIONS FROM ZARETA, Nan mounted a flight of stairs. She rather "felt" Zareta was close behind her, because the dancer moved so lightly her feet made no sound.

Through a poorly lit hallway and then up another flight of steps, and a third, Nan climbed at Zareta's command. At last she was told to halt. The dancer came from behind and rapped sharply on the panel of a closed door. From beyond came a confused murmur of conversation. The door was opened and Zareta entered, beckoning to Nan to follow.

Just beyond the threshold Nan beheld a giant negro standing at one side. In his hand was an unsheathed machete, a wicked razor-sharp knife used by the natives for hacking a path through the jungle or harvesting sugar-cane, but on occasions turned to less peaceful and bloodier uses.

Her heart sank. As she climbed the steps, Nan had been casting about in her mind for some possible avenue of escape. Her position was fraught with peril, she knew, although just what fate was in store for her she shuddered to consider.

"Wait here! You will be called when needed!"

Zareta, without wasting even a glance on her prisoner, glided across the small room they had entered and disappeared through a doorway opposite.

Nan stood quietly. She could feel the beating of her heart. If it had not been that her enemy was a woman, Nan knew she would have fainted with terror, but she stubbornly refused to show feminine weakness before Zareta.

The tall negro pointed with his shining machete to a chair against the wall. Nan sat down in it, her hands folded in her lap, in order to calm their trembling. She saw that the giant guard was watching her like some huge dog eyeing a mouse on which it is about to pounce, a blood-lust in his heavy lidded eyes with their smoldering pupils. There was something familiar in his appearance to her; and then she was sure that this was the man who had overpowered her in her apartment.

She drew the long coat which covered her cream negligee more closely about her. The room was warm, but Nan felt as though she had been chilled to the bone.

She suddenly looked up, conscious that someone was staring at her, and looked into the green eyes of Zareta.

The dancer, without speaking, raised her hand and beckoned to Nan to follow. She nodded to the negro guard, who fell into line behind the prisoner as Zareta led the way.

At first glance Nan thought the adjoining room, which they entered, was empty. Then she saw the sparkle of two long steel blades, points resting on the floor, and behind them the evil black faces and massive figures of two more guards. There was no one else in the place, yet she had the impression that many eyes were watching her—as though the walls themselves could see her, could gloat over every sign of fear that she revealed, and revel in her suffering.

The room was filled with flickering light. Nan turned toward the source of this weird illumination—long tapers at the far end of the room—and only by biting her lips until the blood came was she able to repress a scream of horror.

The tapers were arranged about the edge of a broad low table, which was covered with a red and white checker cloth, not unlike the checkered table cloths used in the rural districts. But what struck terror into Nan's heart was a pyramid about three feet high on the table. It was composed of grinning skulls.

She would have liked to close her eyes and shut out the hideous sight, but was held fascinated by the very gruesomeness. Clustered around the pyramid of skulls, she noticed other human bones, and a pick-axe and spade, the symbols of the gravedigger.

Toward this barbaric altar—for such Nan immediately grasped it to be—Zareta led her. Then Nan understood why the dancer had made no sound when she walked. She was bare-footed.

Before the altar they halted. Zareta raised her hands high above her head and began to utter a low chant in a strange tongue.

When she had finished her incantation, Zareta turned and faced her prisoner.

"Kneel!"

Nan grew rigid. "I won't!" she said defiantly.

Zareta's brows shot up; then she nodded to the guard behind Nan. His powerful hands closed upon her shoulders and the helpless girl was forced to her knees upon the floor. Zareta smiled, a thin-lipped cruel smile, and spoke in a tone that was bristling with malevolence.

"A word from me—and you would die this minute. No one would ever find out what had happened to you, for no one knows where you are except my faithful followers, sworn to allegiance by the blood oath of the *culte des mortes!*"

She paused to note the effect of words upon the kneeling girl, and then went on, her voice soft and sinister.

"But I do not choose to have you die. Dead you would but supply another skull for the altar. Alive you can help me in my purpose."

Nan's hopes were momentarily raised. She had begun to despair of ever escaping from this dreadful place. But Zareta's next words dashed her spirits once more.

"If you do as I bid, if you speak only the truth and tell me what I wish to know, then in due time you will be free to go your way, unharmed. If not—" The dancer's pause was eloquent with menace.

"You know, of course," Zareta said abruptly, "that you were overpowered with a little-known tropical drug, which possesses a powerful hypnotic action. It destroys all ability to resist, it crumbles the will, and, unfortunately, it destroys the power of speech and the faculty of coherent thought.

"The amount given you was very small. A sufficiently large dose would destroy forever your mind. It would place you among the living dead, beyond the hope of any antidote, a woman with a body that could move and obey the will of a master, but a woman with a soul that was dead! Do you understand?" she asked fiercely.

Nan was silent, struck mute by the ghastliness of the picture Zareta was painting so vividly. The dancer beckoned to one of the two negro guards who had been in the ritual chamber when Nan entered, and spoke a few words to him in the strange patois.

He disappeared through a doorway at the back. A few seconds later Nan heard shuffling footsteps, and as she turned to see what new horror this fiend in feminine form had prepared, Zareta exclaimed:

"Behold! That is the fate in store for you, unless you do as I say!"

Nan involuntarily cringed as she saw the figure that was moving across the room. It looked more like a corpse than a human being that was living. The face was a dirty white, the eyes those of a dead person, staring and unfocused.

There was no doubt that the apparition was—or had been at one time—a woman, probably from the features, Nan thought, a mulatto. The hideous thing was dressed in woman's clothes, its black hair was long and stringy, hanging about the expressionless face and accentuating its pasty skin.

"Go!" Zareta commanded. The figure turned without a word and shuffled back through the door by which it had come in.

"That," Zareta said, turning back to the kneeling, terror-stricken girl, "is a *zombie*."

Nan had never heard the name before, but she realized that this wretched creature was somehow a victim of Zareta's evil designs.

"What—what do you want of me?" Nan asked. Her tone was resigned. She seemed to have accepted whatever Zareta might have in store for her.

The dancer gazed fixedly at her for a long time. Suddenly she broke the silence, her question shooting out with a crackle.

"Who killed Carter?"

Nan was stunned. This was entirely different from anything she had anticipated. For a moment she was puzzled as to who was meant by Carter. Then she recalled the tall man with whom she had danced at the Gayety Grotto—the man who had been slain by the gunmen.

"Do—do you mean Mr. Carter—of the Grotto?"

"Don't pretend innocence!" snarled Zareta. "Who else would I mean? You lured him to his death—put the finger on him. Now, damn you—tell me who handled that machine gun. And who were the others in the car with him?"

Zareta had become like a mad woman—like a reincarnation of one of the furies. Nan shrank from her in fright.

"I tell you I don't know!" she screamed. "I never saw the man before last night in my life! I never saw him after he left the dance floor!"

"You lie!" Zareta shrieked, beside herself with rage. "You lie! See! You have red hair!" She reached out a long slender hand, normally a graceful beautiful hand, but now knotted and clutching till it resembled a talon. She seized Nan's hair. "Why didn't you leave with him? Why? I'll tell you. Because you wanted him to die—shot down like a rat!"

Nan was terrified and bewildered, more than ever convinced that she had fallen into the hands of an insane woman, a maniac doubly dangerous because of the strange power she wielded over the members of this savage cult.

The dancer's manner underwent a sudden change. She grew deadly calm, and her very calmness seemed to carry a more sinister peril for the girl kneeling on the floor than had her raging fury.

"Very well. You have had your chance," Zareta said evenly. "It will make no difference in the long run. Your silence will protect no one. You underestimate the *culte des mortes*. Our members are far and wide throughout the cities. In the hovels and dives of the slums, operating elevators in the palatial apartments of Park Avenue, working as porters in the financial district. It is only a question of time—"

Nan gave up hope of convincing this wild fiend of her innocence. "It's true. I swear to you I know nothing about the killing of that man," she said.

Zareta appeared not to hear her. The dancer walked to the low altar with its flickering tapers that cast the ghostly shadows about the room. She lifted an oddly-shaped bottle, more of a jug in shape. Nan noticed that it was ornamented with skulls and twining snakes. For a second time Zareta faced the mound of skulls. She held the jug before her, as a pagan priestess might have held a chalice of blood out to an idol as an offering and again began a strange incantation.

Then she took from the altar a small box. She flipped back the lid and drew from it a shiny metal and glass object. Nan recognized it as a hypodermic needle of unusual size, and the incongruity of a modern medical instrument in the midst of this barbaric proceeding struck her.

Slowly, deliberately, Zareta filled the needle from the contents of the skull and snake-adorned bottle. Then, when she had carefully replaced it on the altar, she turned toward Nan. The dancer's eyes were narrowed until the pupils glinted like tiny emeralds between the long lashes.

"It is your last chance," Zareta hissed. "In another minute you will be among the living dead."

But Nan did not answer. Her taut nerves had snapped at last, and she was lying in a huddled heap upon the floor of the ritual chamber. Zareta looked at her a second, as though debating what course to pursue, and then nodded to the negro guard.

His black arms reached down and his hands closed about Nan's shoulders. As if her weight were nothing, he lifted the girl's limp body erect.

Zareta advanced a step. She raised the glistening needle.

VIII

MANCHINEEL SAP

AS DETECTIVE LIEUTENANT SPAYNE CLEARED THE SMALL FOYER of Benton McCray's apartment in a bound, he whipped from his pocket his businesslike service revolver. Gun in hand he dashed into the short corridor. It was empty.

The stairway was at the rear, and from the landing below came the sounds of a struggle. Spayne started down the steps.

Coming around a turn in the stairs, he saw McCray locked in mortal combat with a gigantic negro. One of the man's hands was at the throat of his smaller white opponent. The other, raised aloft, was clutching a shining dagger. Around the wrist Ben's fingers were closed in a desperate grip.

McCray was a man of good size in perfect physical condition, but he was no match for his huge adversary. His strength, too, was fast ebbing as the air was cut from his lungs. Slowly but surely the deadly blade was being pressed lower by the enormous black man.

The two men swayed back and forth in their embrace of death. Spayne hesitated for a fraction of a second; he dared not risk a shot in the poorly lit corridor for fear of hitting Ben. But as the struggling figures half turned, the detective leaped down the few intervening steps.

His gun swung in a swift arc. There was a heavy thud as its butt crashed against the base of the big man's skull. Without a sound, the negro crumpled in a heap; the dagger clattered to the floor beside the stairway carpet.

Ben leaned limply against the wall gasping for breath. Spayne, with methodical thoroughness, slipped a pair of handcuffs from his pocket and snapped them about the unconscious man's wrists. The bracelets adjusted, he turned to Ben.

"All right?"

McCray nodded. "Yes—yes," he said heavily. "But you got here just in time. He almost had me. Thanks."

"We'd better get him up to your place quick!" Spayne said. "There's no need of having a lot of curious tenants butting in."

It was a difficult task lugging the heavy body of the black man up the steep steps, but at last, breathless and perspiring, Spayne and Ben managed to get him to Ben's apartment and stretched out on a divan.

"We'll see what this black boy has on him," the detective muttered, and began a systematic search of the recumbent victim of his revolver-butt, while Ben watched him.

In one pocket he found a small roll of bills and some change, which he carefully replaced. There were no papers of any kind, no means of identifying the unconscious figure. Then the detective's experienced fingers found something which interested him. He unbuttoned the top buttons of the fellow's shirt.

"That settles it!" The detective straightened up and tossed on the table a duplicate of the *ouanga* which Ben had dissected a short time before. "It was hanging around his neck on a string. This guy belongs to the hoodoo crowd, all right!"

"Voodoo," Ben corrected him with a forced smile.

"They'll think it's hoodoo, when I get through with them," Spayne growled.

He turned again to his search, running his hands over the black man's body and again going through the pockets.

"Not much on him," Spayne said, disappointment in his voice. "All told, he seems to have had some money, that there charm, his knife and this!"

He handed McCray a small phial, about the size of a short pencil stub. "This was in the little match-pocket of his coat."

The phial was of metal with a glass stopper, Ben observed, as he turned it over curiously in his palm. He tried the stopper. It yielded to slight pressure and he withdrew it. Unable to see inside the container, he raised it tentatively to his nose. With a quick motion he replaced the stopper. His expression was puzzled as he quickly pulled out his handkerchief and pressed it to his nose.

McCray turned and walked swiftly from the room. Spayne watched him with surprise, mingled with alarm, and then followed. Ben was in the bathroom bathing his nose with cold water. He glanced up as the detective appeared in the doorway and made a wry face.

"I should have had more sense," McCray grumbled.

"What's the matter?"

Ben dried his nose tenderly with a towel before answering. "It just about burned this useful organ off my face," he muttered. "Unless I'm greatly mistaken, that little phial contains manchineel sap."

"What's that?"

Ben repeated. "The manchineel tree," he explained, "is the deadliest of all tropical poisons. Its fruit resembles a small crabapple, and the sap is so virulent that a couple of drops or less on the tongue causes instant death. Even falling on the skin, it makes sores that are difficult to heal and sometimes are fatal."

"My God! It's lucky you didn't try to taste the stuff!" Spayne exclaimed.

They returned to the other room. Ben took the phial with its venomous contents gingerly from the table and slipped it in his pocket, first making sure that the stopper was secure.

"We'll let the city toxicologist look at this and determine if I'm right in my guess," he said. "But I'm sure I am. The manchineel tree grows in Haiti, in spite of a determined effort to exterminate it. So it's just the sort of poison this fellow here would use."

He looked at the still figure of his enemy lying on the divan, hands held together by the bright steel handcuffs. For several minutes McCray stood in silence, his brow wrinkled.

"Spayne," he said finally, turning to the detective who had been watching him intently, "the way I figure this out is this: Our unconscious visitor here sneaked into this place with the intention of smearing some of that poison on articles that I use—glasses, perhaps even such a thing as my toothbrush."

His eyes narrowed. "It seems this gang of murderers isn't wasting any time in carrying out the threat of the match cross!" Then he said, "I'm wondering what we'd better do with him."

"Why not try giving him a good splashing with cold water and try to bring him around? This guy knows all about the gang. We'll make him talk."

McCray shook his head. "I doubt if you can."

"I've made some pretty tough customers open up and sing like canaries in my day," the detective replied meaningly.

"No doubt," Ben agreed, "but this bird here would suffer the torture of hell before he'd squeal, because he's a lot more afraid of the vengeance of his own gang than he is of anything the whites can do to him. Don't forget that voodooism is a religion with him. That means his hope of the hereafter is more powerful than his fear of the present."

"I'd like to find out about that, but whatever you say goes," Spayne said reluctantly.

"There's just one thing to do, that I can see," McCray said decisively. "We'll tie him up and keep him here. We don't want to take him to the police station—because we've got to keep Nan's name out of the papers."

McCray left the room and after scouring around in the kitchenette and closets returned with two heavy trunk straps and a reel of heavy fishing line.

"These ought to do the trick," he said.

They set to work and in a few minutes the huge negro was firmly lashed to the divan. The fishing line, wound around and around him, made McCray think of the illustration in his boyhood copy of *Gulliver's Travels*, where the giant Gulliver is captured by the Lilliputians while he sleeps.

"That'll hold him," the detective said. "What's next?"

"First we'll slip around to the garage and I'll get my car. We're going to have to cover quite a little ground and there's no use bothering with taxicabs."

"Suits me," Spayne agreed.

"Then we run up to Harlem and try to find this Bruno Le Roy and get on the trail of that fellow Louis. After that, if we don't do any good up there, I want to visit the Grotto."

"Won't be anybody there at this time. They don't open until about eleven at night."

"I know. But that's just one of the reasons I want to go there."

"Check," Spayne said. "Then, if you don't mind, I'd like to slip down to the City Morgue."

"What for?" McCray asked in surprise.

"I'd kind of like to take a look at the dame who was killed by the fire truck, if the body's still there. If it isn't I'd like to find out who claimed it."

Ben shrugged his shoulders. "We'll go there afterwards," he said. "Just a minute."

He walked from the living room to his bedroom. From the bottom drawer of his dresser he removed a flat, efficient-looking automatic, which he slid into his hip pocket. Then he put several extra clips in his coat pocket and rejoined Spayne.

"Well," he said, "let's be on our way!"

The two men left the living room and passed through the foyer into the corridor. As the door closed behind them, the giant negro, a cruel smile twitching the corners of his nostrils, slowly opened his eyes.

IX

WHAT MINK KNEW

BY THE TIME SPAYNE AND MCCRAY HAD SWUNG ONTO FIFTH AVENUE and headed toward the park in the latter's roadster, it was well along in the afternoon. Already traffic was jammed with motorists returning from Sunday outings in the country and their progress was slow.

At Fifty-ninth Street, Ben swung into the park drive, and they began to make better time. When they drew near their destination, Ben pulled off Lexington Avenue onto a side street.

"We'll park the car here," he said, "and approach the place on foot. Nothing like plenty of precautions."

"Good plan," Spayne replied.

They made their way along the sidewalks, crowded with colored children and adults, with now and then a white face. Up Lexington they walked.

"Here we are," McCray added in a low tone, glancing up at a number above a grimy entrance. An elderly negro sitting on the stone balustrade watched them curiously as they entered the vestibule and began to scan the bells, only a part of which bore names.

"Not here," Spayne said finally in disgust. "A man named Bruno Le Roy live in this place?" he asked the old man outside.

The negro thought a minute, and then shook his head. "No, sir, I never heard of no Bruno Le Roy around these parts."

"You lived here long?"

" 'Bout six years."

"Looks like we're stumped temporarily," Spayne said in a low tone to McCray. "But we'll try someone else. Maybe we can find somebody who knows this Le Roy." He glanced up the street. "Wait a minute!" the detective exclaimed.

He strode off rapidly. Ben watched him and saw that he was heading for a colored patrolman, who was strolling along about a half a block away. Spayne approached the policeman and McCray saw him flash his detective badge, then engage in earnest conversation. The detective looked in Ben's direction and beckoned to him to join them.

"This is Patrolman Gilmore," Spayne said briefly, when McCray was with them. "He says he knows this Le Roy."

"That's right," Gilmore attested. "A big black fellow, with kind of ivory-colored teeth that stick out when he laughs. He used to live back there where you inquired. But I haven't seen him for some time, so I guess he's moved away. One of the boys at the pool hall was saying Le Roy'd got a good job playing in an orchestra. He's a drummer, I understand."

"Don't happen to know where he works?"

"Lemme see now," the patrolman muttered. "The Cave—or Cavern, or something like that."

"Grotto?" Ben suggested.

"That's it!" Gilmore exclaimed. "That's the place!"

In a flash it came to Ben why he had imagined he recognized the colored musician who beat the drum in such an odd manner for Zareta's dance. The fellow had been the elevator operator in Nan's apartment building, and McCray had seen him on his visits there. He exchanged a meaning glance with Spayne.

"Come on!" he snapped. Then he suddenly turned to Gilmore as a thought struck him. He looked sharply at the colored patrolman as he spoke.

"Do you know anything about any voodoo cult up in these parts?"

"Mister," the policeman said with a nod of his head, "that's something I don't want to know anything about unless I have to. But I can tell you there's voodoo folks up here—all from the West Indies. I'm a Baptist myself and don't hold with them heathen beliefs and especially that voodoo stuff."

"What do you know about them? Do you know where they meet, or who belongs?" McCray asked.

"No, sir. Nobody knows exactly who belongs, and nobody except the members knows where they hold their meetings. All I know is a little talk now and then that I hear. But I'm telling you they're a bad lot. There's nasty rumors about their carryings-on and I'm thinking they ought to come in here with a few reserves and clean 'em all out."

"That might prove to be a pretty hard job," Ben said dryly.

"You're right," Gilmore nodded. "It'd be a harder job then trying to drive the snakes out of a Louisiana swamp!"

Under the kindly mantle of night, with the electric signs giving it an artificial glamour while the darkness hid its shoddiness, the Grotto was not unattractive. But in the hard light of late afternoon the night club appeared as just what it was—the upper part of an old and shabby two-story building, the ground floor of which was occupied by a public garage.

The door leading upstairs, painted futuristically in bright colors which were beginning to appear weatherworn, was closed. Ben tried the knob. It yielded to his touch and he pushed the door inward.

At the top of the stairs they could see a dim light and the two men started up. The light was coming through the open door of a small office, which opened off the top landing. Mink Magnozzi, Carter's partner, was seated at a desk busied with various papers spread out before him.

The night club owner looked up, peering through the doorway, as he heard the steps outside.

"Hello, Magnozzi!" Spayne greeted him.

"Ah, Lieutenant Spayne," Magnozzi replied. "Come in."

Ben and the detective entered the little office.

"I'm just going over the accounts so I will be ready to settle up with Carter's heirs, whoever they are," Magnozzi said, indicating the littered desk with a wave of his hand.

"Don't know if he had any relatives, huh?" Spayne asked.

"It's just like I told you when we were being questioned at the station early this morning," Magnozzi said. "Mr. Carter and I were in business together, but I knew almost nothing about his private life. He had the dough and I had the experience, so we opened up this place. What can I do for you?"

It was McCray who replied. "Mr. Magnozzi, do you know very much about this colored orchestra that plays here? Where they live, for example."

The night club owner appeared surprised. "Why, up in Harlem, I suppose. I know they used to play at the Little Africana, one of those black and white joints up there. When I hired Zareta—and a pretty high salary she costs me, too—she suggested I get them. Said they could give her the right music for her act, and also supply some hot dance stuff. They seem O.K. to me and the customers like them."

"This Zareta and Carter had a little affair, didn't they?" Ben asked suddenly.

Magnozzi hesitated. "Well," he said slowly, "Carter did sort of fall for the dame at first. There's no doubt that she was nuts about him. Then he cooled off all of a sudden. But the cooler he got, the stronger she seemed to be for him. That's the way with some women," Magnozzi added philosophically.

"What was the reason Carter dropped her?"

"Well, he was one of those guys who has a way with women, and you know how they are—fickle. But in this Zareta business, I guess he lost his taste for her when he discovered she was colored."

"Colored?" Ben was plainly surprised at the information.

The night club owner nodded solemnly. "Yeah. She was so light nobody'd suspect it ordinarily, and then she billed herself as Spanish. Both Carter 'n me thought she was Spanish at first."

McCray glanced at Spayne and knew by the detective's shrewd narrowing of his eyes that the same thought was passing through his mind. If Zareta was colored, in all probability she was connected with the deadly voodoo cult. Ben nodded quickly to Spayne, then turned to Magnozzi.

"Much obliged," he said crisply. "We'll be back later perhaps."

"Always glad to see you," the Italian replied smoothly.

When they were again in their car, Spayne broke the silence.

"Get the layout?" he asked sharply. "This Zareta dame was jealous of Miss Collette. She faked the note in the hopes it would get her mixed up in Carter's killing. It didn't work, so she took matters into her own hands. It's plain as the day!" he added triumphantly.

Ben seemed far from convinced. "You may be right," he said. "But if Carter was dead, I can't quite understand why Zareta would be jealous. Then, too, she probably hadn't ever seen Miss Collette before, so had no grounds for suspecting Carter was interested in her, and there's no doubt he frequently danced with different women patrons."

Spayne was taken back, but only for a moment. "Don't forget that Carter told Miss Collette she looked like some dame he *was* interested in."

It was McCray's turn to be taken back. He was silent for a while, then shook his head. "I can't agree with your theory," he said. "Even if Zareta was jealous of Miss Collette, either because she thought Carter was interested in her or mistook her for someone she knew he had fallen for, I don't think that's a strong enough motive for what's happened."

He slipped the roadster in gear. "I'll take you down to the Morgue, and drop you there. I'm going back to my apartment and see how our prisoner is. Perhaps by now he might be in a mood to talk, though I'm not so hopeful on that score."

"All right," Spayne agreed. "After I do my business and drop in at headquarters, I'll phone you. Then we can lay our plans for tonight."

"You might take this and see that it gets to the city toxicologist," McCray suggested, taking the metal phial from his pocket and giving it to the detective. Spayne nodded.

It was almost dark when Ben drew up in front of his apartment, after leaving Spayne at the City Morgue, found a parking place and went in, after noticing that there were no lights in any of the front apartments.

The hall, however, was illuminated and he climbed rapidly up the stairs. Inserting the key, he turned the lock and stepped into the foyer.

A sudden premonition made him reach for the automatic in his hip pocket. But he was a fraction of a second too late. His wrist was seized in an iron clutch and the bullet, as he squeezed the trigger, crashed into the ceiling.

X

SPAYNE FOLLOWS A HUNCH

ALTHOUGH HIS OFFICIAL DUTIES NOT INFREQUENTLY took him to the City Morgue, Lieutenant of Detectives Spayne always entered the house of death with a distinct feeling of aversion. The present instance was no exception.

In the office on the first floor he met one of the coroner's assistants who was in charge. Spayne explained briefly the object of his visit. The other man shook his head.

"Sorry, Lieutenant," he said, "but you're too late. The body was claimed this noon."

"Who claimed it?" the detective demanded.

"A man who said he was her brother came in first and identified her as a Mrs. Lilly Seeley, of Chicago. He sent the undertaker over to get the remains and arrange for burial."

"Who was the undertaker?"

The assistant coroner consulted a small ledger. "Here is it. Milliken Brothers Funeral Home. That's on Tenth Avenue. Wait a second and I'll find out the exact address for you," he added, thumbing rapidly through a telephone directory.

Twenty minutes later a taxicab deposited Detective Spayne in front of the mortuary establishment of the Brothers Milliken. He entered the somber office. A tall rosy-cheeked man in a shiny Prince Albert coat arose to greet him, rubbing his hands together the while.

"Milliken?" the detective asked brusquely.

The other made a small bow. "I am Mr. Harold Milliken, sir. At your service."

"Good!" Spayne exclaimed. "Well, Mr. Milliken, I came here to inquire about the remains of Mrs. Lilly Seeley, which you claimed at the City Morgue today."

"Ah, yes," murmured Milliken, an oily expression flitting across his face. "Mrs. Seeley. A lovely woman—lovely." He became suddenly efficient. "Well, sir, Mrs. Seeley's body was shipped to Chicago. I dare say the train is just about pulling out of the Pennsylvania Terminal right now," he added, consulting a heavy watch, which he drew from his waistcoat pocket.

"Seems I'm too late," Spayne mused. "Well, Mr. Milliken, I suppose you can give me the name and address of the party that retained you to get the body and prepare it for shipment to Chicago."

It seemed to Spayne that a frightened look appeared for a second in the man's eyes. But he recovered his poise immediately. "Well, sir, I don't exactly recall the gentleman's name—"

"Come on! Snap out of this stalling!" Spayne growled. He had suddenly placed the firm of Milliken Brothers. They were the undertakers who had conducted some of the elaborate and gaudy farewells which Gangland had tendered its members who were bumped off in the course of their nefarious activities.

"What do you mean, sir?" Milliken exclaimed indignantly.

"What I say!" snapped Spayne. "I'm from Headquarters"—flipping back his coat lapel—"and either you speak right up, or you're going along with me. I've got one or two things that I think will hold you. For example, we might put you under a high bond as a material witness in the slaying at the cemetery when you were lowering Dutch Brader into his grave. Then—"

"All right, Lieutenant, ask anything you want," Milliken said, his face losing some of its ruddiness.

"Who hired you to look after this Seeley woman's body?"

"Mr. Edward Chidzic."

"Eddie the Eel, huh?" supplemented Spayne.

"I believe some people call him that," Milliken admitted. "Mr. Chidzic came to me and told me there was a body at the City Morgue, identified as that of Mrs. Lilly Seeley, which he wanted me to claim and have shipped to Chicago. He urged on me the advisability of not mentioning this matter, so I hope—" He lifted an eyebrow questioningly.

"Don't worry, Milliken, I won't get you in bad," Spayne assured the undertaker. "I'm much obliged," he added as he started for the door.

The detective's next move was to hail a taxicab and drive to the police headquarters. There he left the small metal phial he had found on the huge negro. Then he stopped in at the Bureau of Identification.

"Hello, Bert!" he greeted the sergeant in charge. "Take a look at these and let me know what you've got."

Spayne laid down the clipping containing the picture of the woman killed in the fire truck accident, and a sheet of paper he had obtained at the morgue.

The latter was the official description of the dead woman, including her finger prints.

Bert looked at them curiously and then disappeared through a door leading into a rear room. He was gone for almost fifteen minutes, and Spayne was just beginning to grow impatient, when he reappeared. He returned the clipping and coroner's memorandum to Spayne, then gave him a number of record sheets for his inspection.

"That's all we've got," he said. "She seems to have stayed away from here most of the time, but she was wanted plenty in other places, wasn't she?"

Spayne whistled. "Plenty is right," he murmured. He took a notebook from his pocket and copied carefully the salient facts about the woman as contained in the police records. Then he thanked the sergeant and made his way thoughtfully from the building.

Outside he hesitated whether to phone McCray or start out hunting for Eddie the Eel. He decided to try McCray first and entered a drug store on the opposite corner. The operator rang the number repeatedly, but there was no response, and finally the detective gave it up.

"He's probably out getting a bite to eat," he said to himself. "Anyway, we won't want to go up to the Grotto again till after eleven when the orchestra's there. Which reminds me I'd like a snack myself. Then'll give McCray another ring."

Spayne's eye roamed down the street until caught by a bright lunchroom sign, which he at once headed for.

Fortified with steak and potatoes and three cups of black coffee, the detective returned to the telephone booth at the drug store. Once more he failed to awaken any response on McCray's phone. He emerged from the stuffy booth with a worried wrinkle between his eyes.

"Seems kind of funny," Spayne muttered to himself. "I told him plain enough I'd phone him. Guess I'll just hop a subway to Times Square and take a look about on a chance of locating Chidzic. Then I'll drop over to McCray's place."

Putting his decision into action, the detective walked rapidly down to the Canal Street station and caught an uptown express. He climbed from underground at Forty-second Street and started west in the direction of what formerly had been one of the most cancerous parts of New York, now, happily, losing some of its evil reputation—Hell's Kitchen.

Spayne was on familiar ground. Every inch of the Times Square and Longacre districts was known to him. He swung north along Eighth Avenue until he came to Forty-seventh Street. There he turned again west, and coming to Ninth Avenue made his way rapidly north again in the shadow of the elevated.

In front of a doorway, which divided a delicatessen shop and a shoe-shining stand, he halted for a second. Then, after a quick glance up and down the street, he entered. Along a poorly lit hall he made his way cautiously until a second door blocked his path. It was locked. Spayne raised his hand and rapped sharply.

A panel slid back and a dark face appeared. After a hasty but keen scrutiny of the man outside, the face disappeared and the door was opened. The detective stepped in. He passed through a small room into a larger one, along one side of which ran a bar.

Besides the porter, who had admitted Spayne, and then followed him, the only other person present was the bartender. He looked up from a paper he was reading as he heard the detective's steps.

"Oh, howdy, Lieutenant," he said. There was no cordiality in his tone, nor was it hostile. Merely indifferent.

Spayne nodded. "Where's the boss?" he asked.

The bartender laid the paper aside. "Not in, Lieutenant."

There was a faint note in the man's voice which did not escape Spayne's experienced ears. "Come on, Joe. Don't lie to me. This is just a friendly visit," he snapped out. The bartender hesitated.

"Listen to me—you!" growled the detective abruptly, a hard look in his eyes. "If this wasn't a friendly visit, I'd move in here with a squad and take the boss, see? And I'd yank this joint right out by the roots, you, your rotten booze and all. Now step!"

The bartender sullenly drew a bunch of keys from his pocket and, selecting one, unlocked a door behind the bar and disappeared from the room. Spayne could hear him climbing a flight of stairs.

"He wants you to come on up," the man said to Spayne, when he reappeared a couple of minutes later. He held the door open while the detective passed through, then carefully closed it.

Up a flight of steps and Spayne entered a room with several tables and chairs in it, at one of which sat a stout, well-dressed man of middle age. Across from him, hunched over the table, was a rat-faced youth with pasty skin.

"Well, it's the Lieutenant himself!" exclaimed the stout man jovially. Spayne noticed the bottle and glasses on the table and was quickly convinced of the source of the joviality.

"Hello, Eddie."

"Meet my friend Bascom," Eddie the Eel said. "And then pour yourself a little drink."

Spayne took the skinny hand Bascom extended and gave the youth a keen appraisal. Full of dope, the detective decided. He declined the bottle, which

Eddie was holding out toward him, and sat down.

"What's on your official mind?" Eddie asked, putting the bottle back on the table with a shrug. "If you're after me, I'm out. If you just want to sit down an' have a nice friendly little visit, I'm in." He laughed foolishly.

"Well," the detective said slowly, "all I want to ask you, Eddie, is how it happens you're so interested in sending the body of Chicago Lil back west."

Eddie looked quickly at Spayne. Then he poured another drink, and after he had tossed it off in one gulp, he spoke.

"I'll give you the straight dope on that, Lieutenant," he said glibly. "You maybe don't know it, but I was out in Chi a couple of weeks ago. I met this dame, and fell for her, see? She agreed to come down here and be my moll. But just like a dame, no sooner does she arrive than she pops out of a taxi and gets herself accidentally killed.

"She doesn't show when she wrote she would. Then I see the paper and her picture, goes down to the morgue and identifies her. Bein' big-hearted, I ships her body back west to her folks. Sent one of the boys along. That's straight, Lieutenant."

It was a plausible story, Spayne decided, but he knew Eddie the Eel too well to believe that it was true—at least not all true.

"I'm satisfied she was *accidentally* killed," the detective replied with significant emphasis, "because it was a fire truck."

"Hell, you don't think I'd bump off my own moll, do you?" Chidzic asked indignantly.

"I'm not saying," Spayne murmured. "All I wanted to know, Eddie, was where you fit into the thing. I happened to go into the morgue and the man in charge had spotted you when you came in and said you were Lil's brother," Spayne lied smoothly. He was not one to get his informants into trouble.

"That's all. Guess I'll be on my way," he added, standing up.

"Wait a minute," Eddie said suddenly, "and Bascom and me'll walk up the street with you, just to show there ain't any hard feelings. My rep can stand it, if yours can," he chuckled.

"The three men descended the stairs together and the porter let them out the lower door into the dim hallway. Spayne let the others precede him, and as they stepped out in the street, he noticed that the porter was following, but paid no attention to the fact.

"Which way you going?" Eddie asked.

"Over toward Times Square," Spayne said.

"Well, we're heading up Ninth Avenue, but we'll escort you to the corner," Chidzic laughed, half-drunkenly.

They halted at the corner. Spayne shook hands with both the men and stood a minute watching them go up the street. He was puzzled by the frank explanation Eddie had offered for his connection with the body of the redheaded woman. But it was too good a story to be the right one, the detective concluded.

"Yet what's his game?" he muttered.

Chidzic and Bascom were walking side by side close to the curb, when Spayne noticed a large closed car pull swiftly up behind them. The rear door was flung open and three figures leaped out. They were large men, Spayne could see, although they were too far away for their faces to be distinguishable.

Eddie and his companion turned in astonishment; the detective saw Chidzic reach for his gat. But he was too late. The men from the automobile bore down upon them and almost before Spayne, his own gun in hand, could dash across Forty-eighth Street, Eddie and Bascom had been dragged into the car.

Spayne hesitated to open fire. After all, he felt no great anxiety about what happened to gangsters. But at that moment a taxi came swinging along and he impulsively raised his hand. The cab halted with squealing brakes.

"Follow that car, and don't let it get out of sight! Don't mind traffic stops! I'm a police detective!" he shouted to the driver as he slammed the door.

XI

"GOATS WITHOUT HORNS"

ZARETA, THE HYPODERMIC NEEDLE LOADED with the horrible hypnotic drug gleaming in her hand, paused to gloat over the unconscious form of Nan Collette, which the big negro guard was holding upright.

"It is the penalty you pay for defying Zareta, *mamaloi* of the voodoo, high *nebo* of the *culte des mortes!*" she gritted between her clenched teeth, disregarding the fact that the girl to whom she addressed her words was beyond hearing her.

"You are the first payment for the death of my beloved Carter," the dancer continued. "But the others shall be called upon to give up their lives in return for his. I swear it by the great god Ybo, that I shall never rest until I have killed all who had a hand in the death of my beloved!"

With deliberate care Zareta reached out and pulled up the sleeve of the loose coat which covered Nan's negligee, baring the girl's white arm. The soft skin contrasted oddly with the black hands of the giant who was clutching her shoulders.

As if enjoying to the utmost every lingering move, the dancer brought the hypo lower and lower. Now it was six inches from Nan's white flesh, now three, two—one! In another second the sharp point would pierce the skin and pour its terrible contents into the body of the helpless girl. A few more seconds and the drug would begin to eat into her brain cells, to destroy her mind forever and doom her to spend her days among the ghastly ranks of the living dead.

The door leading from the anteroom was suddenly flung open and a negro woman, her hands extended in excitement, burst into the ritual chamber.

Zareta turned quickly, drawing back the needle. On her face was a look of maniacal rage at the interruption. The negro woman began to speak in a high-pitched voice in the strange patois that Nan had heard the occupants of this terrible place use.

Slowly Zareta's face softened.

"Yes, you did well to enter and inform me of what has happened," she said. "Now go. I will join you in the big room on the floor below in a moment."

With a bow, the woman backed from the room. Zareta turned to the guard who was holding Nan.

"Take her into the *zombie* dormitory and stand watch over her! I will summon you shortly!" she commanded.

The guard picked Nan up as though she were an infant and carried her swiftly through the door by which the wretched *zombie* had entered but a short time before. Zareta stood silent, her smooth forehead now furrowed with thought. Then, with a quick gesture of decision, she strode from the ritual chamber with the lithe grace of a tigress and passed through the anteroom into the hallway. The other two guards automatically fell into step behind her.

Zareta, the hypodermic in a pocket in the flowing robe she wore, motioned to the guards to wait. Then she slipped through a door into a small room. She placed her eye close to the wall and peered through a peep hole. What she saw caused her to smile with cruel satisfaction.

Benton McCray, his clothes torn and disarranged, was standing in the center of a large room with his hands bound tightly behind him. On each side was a giant black guard, shining machete in hand. In front of McCray, and grinning at him in triumph, was the negro Spayne had felled with his pistol butt.

"Laugh, you grinning black devil!" McCray rasped out, "but you haven't got me down yet!"

Zareta chuckled. "The white fool has spirit. He is a brave man, but it will do him no good. Perhaps if I feed his heart to some of my timid followers it will make them partake of his courage," she mused.

She glided back to the hallway; then, the two guards behind her, she entered the room where McCray was held a prisoner.

Her appearance came as a surprise to Ben, although he already suspected the dancer was a member of the voodoo worshippers from his conversation with Magnozzi. But he was outwardly calm, and Zareta, watching him closely, was obviously annoyed at his self-control. It pleased her better to have her victims cringing and terrified.

"So," she said softly, when she had taken a position directly in front of him and was surveying him from head to foot, "Mr. McCray has decided to honor us with a visit." She laughed harshly.

Ben made no reply. He knew there was nothing to gain by talking. His course was to wait for a fortunate break; at the moment he was helpless.

"I see you have nothing to say," Zareta continued. "Ah, well, a corked jug spills no wine." She turned to the man, who not so long before had been a prisoner in Ben's apartment, and spoke to him rapidly in the foreign dialect.

Ben recognized it at once as Creole, the corrupted form of French used by the native Haitians. Zareta, McCray saw, assumed he could not understand it, and he was careful to maintain a blank expression. But he was easily able to follow what she was saying; during his time in the Marines in Haiti, Ben had become familiar with the patois of the island.

The dancer inquired of the huge negro the circumstances attending McCray's capture. The fellow explained to her, deferentially but with a note of pride in his voice, what had happened.

McCray cursed his own stupidity silently. The fellow, of course, had not come on his poison-planting mission alone. While he and Spayne had been discussing their plans, the man had recovered consciousness, but had craftily played possum. His companion, waiting outside and not far away in an automobile, had seen the detective and Ben emerge from the apartment house.

After some time had passed, he suspected that all had not gone well with the scheme and entered the place to investigate. Coming upon his fellow plotter bound to McCray's divan, he had freed him. The two had then awaited Ben's return. After capturing him, they had decided to bring him to Zareta alive.

"You have done well, O faithful ones," Zareta said in Creole. "You shall be rewarded."

She started to address McCray, but was interrupted by the entrance of an aged man. His light brown skin was heavily wrinkled and his hair and beard were snow-white, but he carried himself erect. Joining Zareta, he turned his eyes, sunk so deeply in their sockets as to be hardly visible, upon McCray.

"This is the man," he said softly. "And the girl?"

The dancer indicated the floor above with a nod of her head. "She is a prisoner in the dormitory of the *zombies*. But for the arrival of this person, she would now be among their number herself."

Ben's heart seemed to stop beating at Zareta's words. He was filled with an almost uncontrollable rage. This heartless woman had planned to condemn Nan to a fate far worse than death! He tried his bonds cautiously, but the cords which held his hands behind his back had been expertly and securely fastened. There was nothing he could do but bide his time, careful to conceal from his enemies the fact that he understood their language.

But Nan was still alive! The thought buoyed him. She was even now in the same building with him, and the sense of nearness gave to McCray an added determination to outwit these merciless savages by his own cunning.

The old man shook his head dubiously. "I have told you, *Maman* Zareta, that it is dangerous to make *zombies* of such people as these. A skull cannot be identified, but the flesh and blood, even without the mind, is something different. It stands there to accuse you, if these American police—"

"Bah, these police! They are stupid!" Zareta scoffed.

"Have you considered that perhaps the woman was not to blame for the death of your Carter?" the old one mumbled. "You have not heard from all our faithful ones yet."

"She is to blame, even though she denies it!" Zareta snapped.

"Perhaps, perhaps," the man replied, with another shake of his head. "But it does not matter now. It is too late. We cannot let these people go now. They know too much. Those who know too much must have their lips sealed forever!"

McCray repressed a shudder. The old man's words had closed the door on the last hope he had held that they might be freed if Zareta could be convinced that neither Nan nor he had any part in the murder of the night club owner.

Zareta became thoughtful. At last she addressed the aged negro.

"If you think it imprudent, O wise one, to make these prisoners *zombies*, what do you suggest?"

"You," the man replied, "are the high *nebo*. I am but a lowly *bocor*, versed in the black magic and skilled in counsel. Yet if I am to give advice, it is that tonight is the night of the full moon."

"Yes—go on," Zareta urged.

"It is a night when Damballa Ouedda should be appeased."

The trend of the old man's conversation was becoming clear to McCray. Damballa Ouedda was one of the old African gods, the worship of whom had been brought to Haiti by the slaves and interwoven with the voodoo rites.

And Damballa Ouedda was one of the gods to whom blood sacrifices were made—chickens, calves, goats—but occasionally, if the tales Ben had heard in Haiti were true, a human life was offered up to this barbaric deity.

"And you believe—" Zareta paused.

"It is my counsel that the sacrifice of a goat without horns would please Damballa Ouedda and make him smile on our plans," the old *bocor* said.

A goat without horns! Ben knew what that meant. Human beings. And he had no doubt the old man was referring to himself and Nan, and the black's next words confirmed his fears.

"Besides," he said, "I have need for the corpses of a white man and a white woman. There are certain *ouangas* I am preparing that require parts of their bodies. A dried piece of the heart brings courage to the wearer of a charm, if the heart come from those who have been brave. These two seem possessed of courage," he added.

"They are brave because they do not understand," Zareta sneered. "But no matter. I shall heed your counsel. As the moon fades from the morning sky, these two shall pour out their life-blood in honor of Damballa Ouedda!"

The old man nodded approval. "Let the sacrifice take place in the *houmfort* in the country," he suggested. "Damballa Ouedda does not like the cities. He is at home among the trees and bushes, in the open places beneath the white moon."

The mention of the *houmfort*—the name given to the mystery house or temple of the voodoo—convinced Ben that these fiends had another headquarters somewhere beyond the confines of the city. He was gradually beginning to realize the widespread influence and power of the gruesome cult, and the knowledge filled him with despair and desperation.

Zareta's eyes smoldered. "So be it," she said. Then she turned to the guards and began to issue orders rapidly in Creole, the tongue in which she and the old man had been conferring.

All but one of them left the room to do her bidding, to prepare for the departure for the *houmfort*. The one black remained stolidly on guard beside Ben.

Zareta turned to McCray and addressed him in English. "So, Mr. McCray, Papa Henri and I have decided to—take you and the beautiful Miss Collette for a ride into the country. Ah, yes, for a ride." She gave an ugly laugh.

XII

ESCAPE

BLINDFOLDED AND FIRMLY BOUND, BENTON MCCRAY SAT QUIETLY in the back seat of the car. The shades on the windows had been lowered and on either side of him, ever alert, sat one of the huge black guards, of whom Zareta seemed to be surrounded by a great number.

Any hope that he might catch a glimpse of Nan had been crushed when the blindfold had been affixed to his eyes. But the knowledge that she was being taken to the same destination that he was, tempered McCray's wretchedness. If they were near together, there was always the chance that he might break loose and save her from the hands of this inhuman cult.

After what seemed more than an hour, the car turned off the pavement. The noise of the tires on gravel apprised Ben that they were taking to the byways. They were in the country, he realized by the odor of the fields and trees that came to his nostrils.

Ben decided they were headed into Westchester, because he imagined if they had crossed one of the bridges to Long Island he would have been aware of it.

The car came to a sudden stop. There was a low murmur of voices; he could hear the door at the back of the automobile open.

"Get out!" One of the guards uttered the guttural command, and prodded him. He moved forward and a heavy hand was laid upon his arm to help him alight. His feet on the ground, McCray waited quietly for the next move of his captors.

They led him forward—like a lamb to the slaughter, Ben thought grimly—and up a few steps. The next minute he realized they were indoors.

They started to climb stairs. One, two, three flights McCray counted. After that along a short hallway and his feet stumbled over a door jamb. He was given a push and fell heavily to the floor. The door was closed and he heard the click of the lock.

Dazed and bruised, Ben lay quietly. Almost at once the door was opened again. He felt someone seize his ankles and begin to wind heavy cord about them. He was to be trussed up, unable to move about.

"The devils took no chances," McCray muttered as the door again was shut and locked.

He strained at his bonds. But they were firm and although he managed to work himself upright and could still bend his knees freely, that seemed at the moment the extent of his freedom of action. He tried to work his wrists behind his back. They were held tightly together by the cords, but he discovered with a sense of hope that he could wiggle his fingers.

Yet try as he would, McCray failed to bend his wrists sufficiently for his groping fingers to reach the bonds. At last, exhausted and despairing, he dropped back. His shoulders ached from the effort he had put forth and he rolled on his side to ease the pain.

He felt something hard press against his side. At first he was puzzled, then he suddenly realized what it was. The negro guards had searched him for possible weapons, had taken his pocket knife away, but had left the rest of his possessions in his clothes. The object he now felt was his pocket lighter resting in the pocket of his coat.

Hope flamed anew in Ben's heart. It was a chance, though a faint one.

Fortunately his coat was unbuttoned, and little by little, so slowly that at times he almost gave up in despair, Ben worked the coat around in back. His fingers clawed at the cloth till the tips were sore.

At last he was rewarded. The lighter between his first two fingers came from the pocket and dropped to the floor with a faint clink.

McCray wormed his way toward the little metal contrivance. It seemed an hour to him, although it was actually only about five minutes, before he recovered it. This time his fingers pressed it against his palm and his thumb rested on the little lever at the top.

He pressed down. There was a click, but that was all. Again he snapped the flint. Although he could not see because of his blindfold, this time McCray could feel the heat of the flame.

He held the lighter as far from his body as possibly. He realized there was a chance he might set his clothing afire and perish miserably in the flames. But it was no time to count chances. He managed to set the burning lighter on the floor.

Then began the most difficult part of his task—to place his bonds so that the flame would ignite them. He moved slowly, the heat alone for his guide. For a second he lost his balance and then recovered it with a start of agony. The fire had seared his hand.

More slowly he groped around, trying to locate the lighter, and he had almost decided it had gone out before his cautiously moving hands again felt the glow. He burned himself again and again, but gritted his teeth. Finally his perseverance was rewarded. His nostrils detected the acrid odor of smoldering hemp.

The pain in his wrists from the heat and the burns was almost unbearable, but with his freedom in sight McCray steeled himself. Just when he felt that he had to give up, the cord began to yield. He strained his forearm muscles. The strands parted and he was free.

He snatched the blindfold off; then bound his blistered and stinging wrists with strips of his handkerchief. A few minutes work and his ankles were loose. He stood up, aching from the strain and the cramped position he had been forced to maintain. But he was filled with a wild exultation.

McCray looked around him. Through two windows a pale eerie light from the moon filtered in. He could see he was in a small circular room with a conical ceiling.

It was in a cupola of some sort, Ben decided. He walked softly to the door and placed his ear against it. He could hear no sound; the silence seemed ominous. He tried the knob, but the door was locked. Retracing his steps, careful to allow no loose board to betray his hard-won freedom, he crossed to one of the windows.

Outside it was quite light from the moon's rays. He could see that he was at the top of a large house set in the midst of a wild and rugged country. Far off he made out a flickering light. But it might well be miles away, he knew. In between were dark patches of woodland, and immediately around the house itself the trees were dense, the shrubbery crowding to the very foundation of the structure.

"Westchester, all right," McCray muttered. He knew there were many spots within a relatively short drive of New York in Westchester county of equal wildness and desolation.

He pushed up the window silently. Below was a sheer drop of three stories. He leaned from the window and turned his eyes in both directions, but only the edge of a sloping roof was visible. He saw that his surmise that he was in a cupola room had been correct.

The other window proved more promising. It was only about four feet above the shingled roof. He let himself over the sill carefully and dropped to his hands and knees on the shingles. Then he slid slowly down until his feet rested in the gutter pipe.

Noiselessly Ben began to work his way along the edge of the roof. The house was in bad repair he noticed. Frequently he was obliged to cling squirrel-like to the rotting shingles, when he came to places where the gutter sagged, or was missing entirely.

He had almost completed the circuit of the roof, and was surprised at the extent of the house. So far there had been nothing that would help him to climb down from his lofty perch; it almost seemed that he had exchanged one form of prison for another.

Suddenly his sharp eyes detected a dark line running from the gutter up the roof to one of the chimneys.

"A lightning rod," Ben thought. "I'd almost forgotten there were such things."

He inched along until he could seize the stout iron rod with his hand. It seemed to be firm, but he followed it along its length to the chimney where he found it was anchored into the brick with a heavy iron staple.

Then Ben slid back carefully to the roof edge and looked over. He could see down about two stories; below that was an abysmal gloom in the shadow of the trees.

After pausing a moment to adjust the bandages about his burned wrists, McCray set his jaw to stifle any cry from the pain he knew his next move would cause him, and slowly let himself over the cornice. His fingers closed about the lightning rod.

Halfway down the rod pulled loose from its fastenings on the side of the house and Ben swung dizzily in space. His knees closed around the loose rod; it appeared certain that he would be dashed to death below. But he continued his slow descent. The rod held and at last his outstretched toes felt the firm ground.

He slumped to the earth and lay there for several minutes recovering his breath and his strength. Then he slowly got to his feet and peered about. It was impossible to see more than a few feet away in the deep shadows, but where the moonlight broke through the foliage were bright patches—almost like spotlights. Carefully avoiding the moonlit spots, Ben began a careful advance.

There were no lights in the big house that he could see and Ben concluded that the windows were all heavily shaded. But he was sure in his mind that his enemies were within—and Nan. The thought of his peril made him clench his hands, in spite of the excruciating agony the gesture cost him.

XIII

BENEATH THE ALTAR

MCCRAY BEGAN A CIRCUIT OF THE PLACE, pausing at each step to listen. There was no sound except the soughing of the breeze through the leaves, and from afar the ghostly hoot of an owl. McCray was hunched over now, examining carefully the stone foundation of the building. At last he found what he was seeking.

A cellar window, not more than a foot high and begrimed with dirt and cobwebs, met his touch. He dropped to his knees and pushed against it, but it held fast. Again he tried, bracing his foot against the lower part of the frame. He was running desperate chances, Ben knew, for the window might give way with a clatter of glass that would bring the whole black pack down upon him.

Little at a time the window yielded to his efforts, until, with a faint trickling of loose cement to the cellar floor, it swung inward and up. He felt on the other side of the frame and found a small hook, with which he fastened it open. Then he squirmed through the opening feet first, and, hanging by his hands, dropped to the cellar floor.

He was in inky darkness. He snapped his lighter and let it burn for a few seconds until he could get his bearings. Everywhere he saw dust and cobwebs. At one time the room had been a vegetable cellar he imagined, for he could see in the flickering light that it was lined with bins. Before he was again in the dark, Ben noticed an open door and groped his way toward it.

Guided now solely by his hands held out before him and cautiously exploring the ground with his toe before placing a foot down, he moved ahead. He had advanced about ten feet into the second basement chamber when he decided to risk another brief burning of the little pocket lighter. A strong odor of quicklime had stirred his curiosity and given him a feeling of uneasiness.

As the flint struck fire he looked around. An involuntary gasp burst from his lips and his flesh seemed to creep at the sight which met his eyes. He lifted his feeble light above his head, and peered in horror.

In three shallow boxes, half-covered with lime, he saw the bleaching bones of human skeletons. Not far away was visible a pile of human bones, although he saw, with surprise in the second before the light went out, that it included no skulls.

He was in the charnel house of the *culte des mortes!*

Benton McCray was a man of strong nerves. He had served in the Marines and seen violent death many times. But the full realization of his position—alone and unarmed in this gruesome mortuary, with the gang of murderous fanatics above him in the house, Nan in their power. As he grasped all this, it was with the strongest effort of will he had ever exerted that he controlled himself. For an instant he was on the verge of rushing from the place, screaming like a madman.

Once more he risked the light, and made his way with all haste from the place. The next room he entered was the furnace room. Ben could see the outline of the heating plant, its many branching pipes giving it the appearance of some huge and grotesque spider.

He must be somewhere near the stairway that led to the upper part of the house, he knew, and a little later he made out the first few of the stairs extending out behind the furnace. Silently he climbed. At the top step his way was barred by a closed door; he paused, crouching low. From beyond the portal came a low mumble of voices.

McCray was unable to distinguish what was being said. A minute later the sound of talking ceased and he could hear the sound of the speakers moving. He tried the door cautiously. It was unlocked.

Inch by inch, so slowly that it seemed scarcely to move, he pushed the door open and stepped out of the cellar. He was in a small hallway of some sort, beneath the slope of a stairway. The steps to the upper floor, he assumed. The only light came from a sputtering candle set in a bracket in the wall.

He started forward, flattening himself against the wall. It was evident that his escape from the cupola room had not been discovered; his enemies' confidence in the bonds they had placed on him brought a sardonic smile to Ben's face.

Moving cautiously into the next room, a larger and almost square hall, from which the stairway led upward, Ben suddenly drew back into a shadowy corner. In the vestibule on the far side he had seen the form of one of the black guards.

Muttering a silent prayer of thanks for the candle illumination of the place, which made protecting shadows, Ben waited. The guard made no move, and Ben ventured to look around. He saw he had stepped into a recessed doorway.

His hand found the knob and he pushed the door open. Then, with a quick glance at the negro in the vestibule, he glided into the room and closed the door softly.

He was in a high-ceilinged apartment of unusual size. Like the rest of the house it was lit with candles, and, Ben noticed in his first rapid survey, almost entirely unfurnished. At the opposite end, set in a wide bay window, he saw a low table, checkered cloth and pyramid of skulls—the altar of the *culte des mortes*.

With a feeling of repulsion, Ben approached the barbaric arrangement and examined it more closely. Resting on the table, which formed the base of the altar, was a ring of tall flickering tapers. Behind them he saw a crude statue, carved from wood, and representing a hideous human figure caressing a coiling snake.

On either side were various bottles and jugs—drink for the god, Ben decided—and several bowls contained some sort of ground meal.

But what held McCray fascinated for a second was the sight of a huge white bowl and beside it two machetes of unusual size. And Ben realized with a shudder that these were the sacrificial blades, and the bowl was the receptacle into which would gush the life blood of the wretched victims offered up in honor of this heathen deity.

"They've got everything ready," he muttered to himself. "But one of their 'goats without horns' may butt into their schemes yet," he added grimly.

His spirits, however, began to climb. Here at least was the first successful step in his plans. A weapon! He picked up one of the machetes. The delicacy of its balance for a knife of such size filled him with admiration. And the feel of the ivory handle in his palm brought a tingling sense of confidence and hope.

McCray started to move toward the door, but voices coming from beyond brought him to a quick halt. He backed slowly to the altar and stood tense and listening, his eyes darting about the room in search of a place to conceal himself.

The next instant the voices drew nearer and the handle of the door turned. Ben dropped to his knees, raised the overhanging edge of the red checkered cloth on the altar table and crawled beneath. He heard the door close and then a voice, which he recognized as that of the old *bocor*, spoke.

"The hour grows late," the magician said, using the Creole tongue. "I have just looked out, and the moon is dropping low in the sky. The time is at hand to begin the services to Damballa Ouedda."

"Yes," came from a voice Ben placed as that of Zareta. "You are right. Everything is in readiness."

"Which one dies first?" the *bocor* asked.

"We will have a double sacrifice," Zareta said. "With one stroke you shall dispatch them both, and their blood will mingle in the offering to Damballa Ouedda. Surely Damballa Ouedda will be pleased that we have provided him with such a sacrifice—and I shall taste of the cup of vengeance," she added softly.

Zareta and the *bocor* approached the altar. Beneath the lower edge of the cloth Ben could see their feet. He noticed that the dancer was wearing sandals of a crude form, such he had often noticed on the natives dwelling in the hills, during his period on the island of Haiti.

Would they notice the absence of one of the sacrificial machetes? Ben held his breath, but, apparently all seemed well to the priestess and her black magician, for she suddenly spoke.

"While you go and summon the faithful from all parts of the *houmfort*, I will order the guards to bring the man-goat and the girl, that they may be present and enjoy the ceremony that precedes their entry into the beyond." She laughed, an inhuman savage sound, that sent a chill through Ben's veins.

XIV

A Ghastly Ceremony

In a few minutes—seconds now—McCray's escape from the room in the cupola would be discovered. He hesitated whether to break forth from beneath the altar and try to force Zareta, the machete at her throat, to liberate both Nan and him, or to sit tight and await developments.

It was unnecessary for him to make a decision, however. At that moment he heard the door open and several persons enter.

It was Zareta who spoke first, and from her words Ben realized that one of the new arrivals was Nan. The others, he assumed, were the guards who had brought her from the room where she had been kept a prisoner since their arrival from the city.

"Come! Let me look closer at you," the dancer ordered. "It is a pity that such beauty must die," she continued sneeringly, "but then Damballa Ouedda loves a beautiful sacrifice."

"You mean—you mean that you are going to kill me?" Nan's voice was firm, but there was a note of disbelief, as though it were beyond her understanding that such things could take place in the midst of a civilized community at this day and age.

"Kill?" Zareta repeated with a hard laugh. "No, no, not that word. Sacrifice. Before the moon goes down that white throat of yours shall pour into the sacrificial bowl your life-blood in honor of Damballa Ouedda. Unless—" She paused, and Ben could feel that her green eyes were boring into the helpless girl before her.

"Unless you have changed your mind and are willing to tell me who killed my beloved Carter!" the dancer added harshly.

Ben gritted his teeth in helpless rage at Zareta's cruel toying with Nan. Her words were a lie he knew from what he had heard of the conversation between the dancer and her *bocor*. It was too late now for these voodoo worshippers to let them go. Regardless of their innocence in the slaying of Carter, Zareta would kill them both to protect herself and her followers from discovery.

"Well?" Zareta suddenly burst out. "Have you changed your mind? Are you prepared to tell me?"

Nan's tone was resigned. "I have already told you. I know nothing about it."

There came from the hallway the sound of hurrying feet. Then the door to the ceremonial chamber was thrown violently open. Ben in his hiding place close to the floor could tell by the feet and ankles visible beneath the checkered cloth that covered the altar that two of the guards had entered. They spoke in excited voices, using the Haitian Creole, which McCray understood.

"He is gone—"

"What?" Zareta exclaimed.

"The white man—he has escaped!"

Breathlessly, almost incoherently, the negroes explained that they had gone to the cupola and discovered their prisoner no longer there. They told of the open window, how they had searched the roof and had finally decided that the *blanc'* had made his way to the ground by means of the lightning rod.

"Fools! Idiots!" Zareta screamed. "May the curse of Ybo be upon you for your carelessness. After him!"

"The white man?" It was Nan's voice.

"Yes, the white man!" the dancer snapped. "Your McCray—but never fear. He will be recaptured!"

A gasp from Nan convinced Ben that up to this moment she had been unaware that he, too, had been a prisoner of the *culte des mortes*. The news that he was near, straining every effort in her behalf, he felt sure would lend her courage in the crisis he saw approaching.

Zareta was almost beside herself. She paced back and forth across the ceremonial chamber shouting orders.

"After him! Turn everyone out of the *houmfort* to search the grounds. He can't go far in the darkness!"

"He hasn't gone far—you're right," Ben whispered to himself, "and before long you'll find it out, you she-devil!"

He resisted an impulse to break from his hiding place, machete in hand, and attempt to hack his way to freedom with Nan at his side. And the realization that they were in a desolate spot far from help checked him. It would be a courageous act, but it would be foolhardy. The odds against them were too great. He must bide his time.

Zareta now was standing at the door of the room shouting encouragement to the voodoo worshippers as they poured from the place like black ants from an ant hill. The noise of running feet in the halls, the sound of many voices gave evidence that the place was occupied by a considerable number of the cult. At least twenty or thirty, Ben imagined.

At last the old *bocor* spoke, addressing his words to Zareta.

"It is a waste of time, *Maman* Zareta," he said quietly, heedless of the hubbub that filled the place. "If you will listen to the words of an old man, I will advise you."

"Speak!" the dancer replied. "I have always found your advice filled with wisdom."

The magician was silent a moment, as though weighing what he was about to say. Then:

"The white is well aware that we still have in our power the woman. He knows, too, that time is moving swiftly." He paused.

"Well?" Zareta urged, a trifle impatiently.

"The white is a brave man. He would not run away to leave the woman to die. He is not far, of that I am certain. Perhaps he may even be concealed within the *houmfort*. Anyway, the precipice—"

Ben silently cursed the old fellow's shrewdness. Zareta seemed to be considering his words.

"What would you have us do?" she asked.

"Recall the faithful. Have them assemble in the chamber here. Leave a circle of guards on the alert about the *houmfort*. Then let us offer up the life of the woman to Damballa Ouedda. After that he will aid us to find the man, and we can shed his blood, too—let it gush into the sacred bowl." He became eager as he made the last suggestion.

"Your wisdom is the wisdom of a hundred serpents," Zareta murmured. "We shall do as you say."

She muttered several low commands to one of the guards in the hall and then rejoined the *bocor*, standing before the altar. Nan, unable to understand the Creole dialect, had missed the meaning of the conversation, Ben realized thankfully. He was filled with wonder and admiration at the brave manner in which she had faced the terrible ordeal of her capture.

Presently from the upper part of the house came the mournful and blood-chilling beat of a *rada*-drum, recalling the followers from their search of the grounds to the *houmfort*.

Gradually the large ceremonial chamber began to fill with the members of the cult. By placing his head almost on the floor Ben was able to obtain a view of the assemblage, at the same time thanking his lucky stars that the light came from the ring of tapers on the altar. This left his hiding place below in total darkness.

There were both men and women, he noticed, the former, however, predominating. They were all colored, ranging from Ethiopian blackness to a pale yellow, scarcely distinguishable from white. On every face was an expression of fanatic intensity.

"A cruel-looking pack," McCray muttered to himself. He made a hasty count of the worshippers, who were beginning to squat on the floor opposite the altar and some ten feet and more from it. There must be about twenty-five, he decided. Probably, with the giant guards, his enemies numbered pretty close to fifty.

Zareta ordered two of her followers to take Nan to one side of the altar. Someone had brought in the three *rada*-drums, inseparable from all forms of voodoo services, and soon, at a word from Zareta, there arose a soft drumming—weird, savage and of that same odd rhythm Ben had noticed at the Grotto.

A barbaric chant, almost childish in its wording, began to come from the throats of the group. It was an appeal to Damballa Ouedda to come down and receive the sacrifice they were about to offer.

Ben could see only the hem of the white robe Zareta was wearing and her bare feet, because she was standing close to the altar. A few feet behind her and to one side stood the *bocor*. Suddenly the chanting ceased. Zareta began a monotonous incantation, whose very sameness was somehow terrifying.

She stopped abruptly and in a low tone commanded that Nan be brought before the altar. Ben could see only the moving feet of the principals in this gruesome rite as all were next to the altar.

"Kneel!" the dancer commanded.

Nan dropped to her knees, her head bent low. Again Zareta started her monotonous refrain. Ben edged his way forward. His face now was only a foot from the bowed head of Nan. He was afraid if he spoke, she might betray his presence, but he had to chance it. It was necessary that she know of his nearness. So at the risk of startling her, he whispered.

"Don't be afraid, Nan. It's Ben. I'm under the altar and armed. In a minute or two I'll come out and we'll try to fight our way to freedom. It's the only chance."

He could see Nan's hand close convulsively at the sound of his voice. But beyond that she revealed no emotion. And the twitching of her hands was not enough in itself to attract attention under the circumstances.

Ben waited with every muscle tightened. Had his whispered warning to Nan been heard? Apparently not, for Zareta continued her incantation for a little longer. Then she spoke.

"The bowl! The knife!"

The moment was at hand. Ben braced himself for his next move, which would launch him from beneath the altar and into the midst of these black fiends. He waited to time his leap perfectly. If his appearance came at just the psychological moments when the voodoo members would be taken sufficiently by surprise almost to imagine him to be Damballa Ouedda himself, there was faint chance his wild plan might succeed.

Zareta was speaking to the *bocor*.

"Take this sacred knife, O wise one. While I hold the bowl, perform your duty!"

The magician stepped forward slightly. In another second he would have felt the gleaming machete, which Ben was gripping in his hand, plunge through his body, but suddenly from outside the ceremonial chamber arose the noise of a violent struggle.

Halted just as he was about to spring forward, Ben saw Zareta and the *bocor* step rapidly back from the altar. The door of the ritual room was thrown open. There was the sound of several voices and then further commotion.

Above the uproar could be heard clearly, in unmistakable gangster accents, one voice.

"What do you black boogies think you're gettin' away with?"

XV

CARTER'S KILLERS

"WHAT DOES THIS MEAN?" Zareta exclaimed in angry tones.

The man who had spoken so loudly before attempted to repeat, but Ben could hear the thud as he was struck full on the mouth by one of the giant guards.

"Silence!" Zareta commanded loudly. The excited chattering of the voodoo worshippers, which had broken out at the interruption of the sacrificial rites, immediately ceased. The room was deathly quiet as she spoke again, this time in Creole.

Ben peered from beneath the altar covering. He could see she was addressing a large negro who was standing beside two white men. Behind, he noticed the shining faces of several of the huge machete bearers.

"Why is that you dare to interrupt the service to Damballa Ouedda?" the dancer demanded sternly.

The man inclined his head deferentially. "Because, oh, *Maman* Zareta! we, your faithful, have found the ones you sought."

"Who is it you have found?"

"The murderers of *M'sieu* Carter, oh, *Maman* Zareta! Behold, they stand before you!"

Ben looked in astonishment at the two white men, both of whom appeared cowed after the blow which had silenced the one's outburst. Both were strangers to him.

Zareta stood with arms akimbo staring at the two white prisoners for several seconds. Then she made a little sign and the group advanced into the room.

Nan had remained upon her knees. As the others came nearer she edged to the altar and her hand reached beneath. Ben's fingers closed upon it with a reassuring grip and the answering pressure set his blood tingling.

"Tell us, faithful one, the names of these men and how you captured them?" Zareta demanded, still using the Haitian Creole dialect.

The big negro touched one of the whites, a stout well-dressed man of middle age, on the shoulder. "This is Edward Chidzic, called by the whites Eddie the Eel. And this"—he tapped the other prisoner, a rat-faced youth who was twitching nervously—"this man is known as Bascom."

A soft whistling sound, almost a hiss, came from between Zareta's tightly pressed lips. "Go on!" she said. The man continued.

"When you, O *Maman* Zareta! commanded that the faithful keep their eyes wide open and their ears alert for clew to the killers of *M'sieu* Carter, the word was spread far and wide. In the slums, in the abodes of the rich, in the offices, in the speakeasies, it was heard and heeded.

"We knew that in time one of the faithful would overhear a careless word. For the whites are not always careful in the presence of those who are serving them.

"And thus it came about not many hours ago that one of our members, a humble but devoted follower, informed me that these two had killed *M'sieu* Carter."

"Who is this devoted follower? How did he find the guilty ones?" Zareta asked.

"He is one Daniel Leon."

"See that he is rewarded."

"It shall be done. Leon was the porter in the speakeasy, which this Chidzic owns and makes his headquarters. This afternoon Leon served drinks to these two whites. In their cups they are talkative. They laugh and boast about what they have done."

"I understand," Zareta murmured. "Is that all?"

The man shrugged his shoulders. "Except that we captured them as soon as they left the place. That was such an easy task, that I scarcely would have mentioned it."

"And why did they kill my beloved Carter?"

"Leon did not know. They had not talked of why, but only how they had killed him and the two others. Chidzic drove the automobile. Bascom pressed the trigger of the machine gun. That is all."

"It is as I thought," the aged *bocor* said to Zareta. "The white woman had nothing to do with it."

Zareta laughed softly, harshly. "You are right. But that is too late to worry about. She must die, because she knows too much. Besides I do not like her. That alone is sufficient reason for her to be sacrificed to Damballa Ouedda."

"It is a good night," the magician chuckled. "We shall offer the white woman and these two white men. Then we shall capture the other white man and he, also, shall pour forth his blood. Surely, Damballa Ouedda will be pleased."

The *bocor's* tone was heartless. Ben pressed his lips into a thin line, and thought to himself that, although they all might die, the cruel magician would be the first to go.

"Come, let us continue with the service!" the *bocor* exclaimed. "We have already made our appeal to Damballa Ouedda. Even now he is waiting for the sacrifices."

"Wait!" the dancer replied. She turned to the two gangsters, who were staring wide-eyed and terrified at the gruesome altar, and addressed them in English.

"Why did you kill Carter?"

Chidzic managed to find his voice, but Bascom, his last "shot" of dope having worn away, was trembling and nerve-shattered.

"Carter? I don't know nobody by that name," Eddie the Eel, an attempt at surly swagger in his voice, replied.

"It is useless to lie to me," Zareta said quietly. "I know all. And because you killed him, you are going to die. But not in the way you would prefer. You are going to be offered as a human sacrifice; you are going to have your throats cut with the sacred machete."

Eddie the Eel was not a coward in the generally accepted use of the term. In a knife fight he was always ready to exchange thrust for thrust. No one was more willing to stand up, blazing gat in hand and shoot it out with the police or rival gunmen. Even had he been taken for a ride by his enemies he would have maintained a sneering attitude of defiance.

But Eddie the Eel was the ignorant product of the gutter. And his ignorance made him fear things he did not understand; and now he was face to face with a barbaric cruelty that far exceeded the viciousness of his own murderous world. His courage crumpled.

The terror of Hell's Kitchen begged for his life—offered fabulous sums. He might have been a frightened schoolboy pleading to escape a whipping for all the bravery he displayed.

Bascom was even more terrified. As the significance of Zareta's pronouncement sank into his addled consciousness, his drug-torn nerves collapsed. He fell to the floor writhing and screaming for mercy. His limbs contorted with the agony of fear.

Afraid that the dope fiend might discover his presence under the altar, Ben crawled as far back into the bay window as possible. There he remained a second, one hand braced against the wall behind him. Suddenly he smiled quietly to himself. It was a chance—by far the best one that had occurred to him, he decided.

After a hasty examination of the altar and the bay window with his fingers, he crept softly forward until he found Nan's hand reaching beneath the altar cover far at one side. He drew her down until his lips almost touched her ear through the cloth.

"When I give you the signal," he whispered, "dive underneath here as fast as you can. Leave the rest to me."

She gave his hand a squeeze to indicate that she had heard him and understood. Ben freed her hand and crawled back until he was in the middle of the front of the altar. Directly before him lay the writhing Bascom. He could see only the lower part of Chidzic, Zareta, the *bocor* and the negro who had brought in the two gangsters.

Behind them, the members of the cult were standing up for the most part, although a few still maintained their squatting attitudes about the big room.

Zareta's voice rang out, cutting icily into the turmoil and pleas the two condemned gunmen were setting up.

"Bind them! If they have no control, we will tie them up like the cowardly pigs they are!"

As two of the guards stepped forward and began to affix strong cords to the two white men, Ben crawled back to where he could whisper again to Nan.

"Count ten," he said, "and then come under here as fast as possible and wait for me. Go to the very back. All right! Now!"

• • •

He made his way back to the center of the altar and crouched. Then with an ear-splitting scream, designed to instill panic into the superstitious voodoo worshippers, he leaped from his hiding place. The long blade of the machete glistened in his hand. At the same moment out of the corner of his eye he saw Nan disappear beneath the altar cloth.

In his first leap from below the table that served as an altar, Ben bowled over the aged *bocor* and Chidzic. The rest of the little group, taken completely by surprise, involuntarily pushed back. He was left with a cleared space of several feet about him.

The members of the cult in the background were speechless with fright for a second, then suddenly set up a great shrieking and wailing, believing the disheveled figure waving the shining blade was Damballa Ouedda himself.

With a quick bound Ben jumped to the altar. The machete circled his head once and then sailed around the ring of tapers. They flew in all directions and went out.

The ritual chamber, in inky darkness, became an inferno of cries and struggling blacks. But Ben knew he had but a few seconds in which to accomplish his purpose. The momentary surprise was quitting the dancer and the magician and they were already shouting loud commands and endeavoring to calm their frightened followers.

Ben took a backward step and his groping hand found what he sought— the wooden image of the snake god. Pulling the handle of the machete through his belt, he grasped the idol and raised it above his head. With all his strength he hurled it.

There was a crash of glass as the heavy image struck the bay window, carrying away the entire frame. Ben once more grasped the machete in his hand, and, kicking in all directions the pyramid of skulls, reached the back of the altar. He braced himself against either side of the shattered window, found a hold for both his toes against the back edge of the altar and pushed.

The altar slid forward a couple of feet, until blocked by the bodies of those in front of it. Nan, her face visible in the pale moonlight that was streaming through the window, stood up.

"Quick! Out the window!" Ben exclaimed. "They might try to shoot and we're a perfect target here!"

She scrambled through the broken window. Ben followed close behind. His fear that one of the guards might be armed with a pistol proved justified. There was a flash behind them, but the bullet failed of its mark.

Then a black form appeared in the window. Ben whirled and the long blade of the machete shot forward. He could feel it sink deep into the body of the pursuing negro, who groaned and then dropped half in and half out of the window.

They were on a wooden gallery that ran alongside the front of the house.

Ben took Nan by the arm and started in the direction away from the front entrance. The sound of the uproar in the sacrificial chamber was lessening, and he knew it was only a matter of seconds before the pack would be in hot pursuit.

"Stick as close to the side of the house as you can, Nan darling," Ben whispered. "Stay right behind me."

Nan dropped in back of McCray, one hand resting lightly on his shoulder, and they made their way as rapidly as possible in the fast waning light of the moon, to the end of the gallery. There a flight of steps led down into the dark shadows. It was a corner of the house.

At that instant a black figure ran into view. The blade of his machete sparkled above his head.

"Back!" Ben exclaimed sharply. Nan dropped back, an involuntary gasp escaping from her lips.

The negro guard saw them. His machete, as he leaped forward, swung sideways and down, as once it must have swung in hacking the tangled jungle.

But Ben was set for him. A spark accompanied the clash of steel on steel. The wicked looking blade of the guard was deflected with a deft twist and went clattering to the ground. McCray lunged forward. With a scream like a wounded animal, the guard sank to the ground in a pool of blood.

"Just like saber practice," Ben said triumphantly, seizing Nan's hand. "Come on!"

They dashed down the steps and across the short space of lawn which separated them from the protection of the heavy shrubbery. Nan clung desperately to his hand as they crashed into the thicket. A crack of a pistol warned them that the chase was on.

XVI

A MEETING

FOR SOME DISTANCE BEN AND NAN, hand in hand, stumbled through the underbrush. There were no more shots. Only an ominous silence came from behind them as they put as much distance as possible between the house and themselves.

Ben, however, knew it was too much to hope for that the voodoo worshippers had abandoned the chase. It was much more probable, he realized, that the blacks were stealthily stalking them, as jungle beasts silently stalk their prey in the night.

They came to a patch of shrubbery that was denser than the rest, and he called a halt. Both were breathing heavily from the exertion of their mad escape. Nan clung to him, her arms about his shoulders.

"Frightened?" he asked, holding her close.

"No," she murmured. "Not so long as I am with you, Ben dear."

They stood motionless, listening sharply for sounds of pursuit. Faintly from a distance they heard the sound of voices, but they were too far off for the words to be distinguishable. Then in the direction of the *houmfort* there was a brief flash of light.

"The fools," Ben whispered. "If they come after us with flashlights, they'll never find us."

The pursuers, apparently, realized that was the wrong method, too, for there were no more flashes. Nothing came to their ears either, except the night sounds of the woods—the rustling of the leaves in the breeze and the occasional call of some nocturnal bird. There was something more sinister in the deathly stillness than there would have been in the cries of a noisy chase.

Nan and McCray stood in the kindly blackness of the clump of shrubbery until they had both recovered their breath. Then he again took her hand.

"We'd better start," he said softly.

They began to move ahead slowly and cautiously. Ben used the machete to feel ahead of them in the darkness, which was growing more intense as the moon disappeared. It would soon be that short period of stygian gloom, which precedes the first rays of dawn; a time when night seems to muster all her forces in a last effort to push back the oncoming day.

He halted suddenly. Then advanced one foot carefully. At once he drew back.

"What's wrong?" Nan whispered.

"We're on the edge of some kind of ravine," McCray replied. "We'd better change our course, because it may drop off in a steep cliff."

They moved to the right, investigating each foot of their way before advancing. This, together with the need for quietness, made their progress slow. From time to time, Ben attempted to move in a direction away from the house. But his groping machete invariably encountered only space as the ground dropped abruptly away.

After covering about a hundred yards in this fashion, Ben called another halt.

"I'm beginning to understand why they seemed to give up the chase," he murmured. There was a note of anxiety in his voice, which Nan did not miss.

"Tell me, Ben dear," she whispered. "After what I've gone through already, nothing can frighten me."

"This cliff probably extends a large part of the way around the back of the grounds—perhaps it just about surrounds the house. I've a hunch they are letting us flounder around in the darkness and only guarding the section where there is no precipice. As soon as it's light, they probably figure, they'll be able to find us."

"You mean—you mean we're trapped?" she whispered.

"Yes."

They stood in silence for several minutes. Then Ben came to a sudden decision.

"Nan," he whispered, "we're going to try to get out by the main entrance in front."

"Whatever you say, Ben dear," she whispered, and pressed his hand confidently.

He stooped down and felt around the ground until he found a spot of soft loam. Scooping up a handful, he gave her half of it.

"Smear this on your face and hands," he said. "It will help to conceal our white skins."

There would be only ten or fifteen minutes more of protecting darkness, he realized, and then dawn would break rapidly. They had no time to lose.

Ben leading the way, they started in the direction he had figured out the house was situated. With utmost caution they advanced, trying to keep from letting any snapping of a twig betray their position.

They came shortly to a small clearing, which they skirted. At the far side their feet encountered a hard smooth surface. Ben placed his lips close to Nan's ear and whispered:

"It's some kind of a walk. We must be getting close to the house. We'll follow it a little ways."

The going was easier now, but they did not relax their caution. Somewhere in the gloom ahead, both knew, were the black machete men, straining to catch sight or sound of them. An encounter with one of the blacks would bring the entire murderous crew swooping down upon them.

Suddenly from right behind them came a sharp, commanding whisper.

"Don't move or you'll be killed damn quick. And keep your mouths shut! You hoodoo rats!" There was a soft triumphant chuckle.

Ben promptly broke the command to keep still with an astonished whisper.

"My God, it's Spayne! This is McCray."

There was a faint gasp of surprise and a second later Detective Lieutenant Spayne had joined them, his powerful figure just barely visible.

"I knew you the minute you pulled that hoodoo crack," Ben said softly.

"Who's this with you?" the detective asked.

"It's Nan—Miss Collette."

"By George, how did you two get way up here in Westchester?" Spayne muttered. Then added, "Wait! We'd better not try to do any more talking here. Follow me."

A little later he paused. "This is all right," he said. "We're almost at the road."

"I thought we were going toward the house from in back," Ben said softly.

"No. You must have gotten lost in the dark. That walk leads from a lodge at the gate to the stables in the rear and misses the house, so Rourke tells me."

"Rourke?"

"Sure. Sergeant Rourke, of my station at one time," Spayne replied. "I picked up Rourke and a squad while I was following a big car with Chidzic and Bascom. Rourke was born in Yonkers and tramped all over this country as a kid. He says this is the old Jared place."

"Is it surrounded by a precipice?" Ben asked.

"You guessed it. Rourke tells me old Jared was sort of queer. He built the place on a hill with steep sides and wherever it needed it he built high stone walls. The only way anyone but a human fly can get in is by the front way."

"Weren't there guards out there?"

Spayne chuckled. "There *were*. Fact is, there still are, but we've got 'em well tied up with their own rope. But what happened to you?"

Ben gave him a rapid account of the terrifying events that had taken place. Spayne interrupted from time to time. "Think of that. The black devils!"

"You say you've captured three of the machete men. I've put two out of the way so far as fighting is concerned. That means there's probably not more than ten or twelve left at the outside," Ben said.

"Well, we're pretty well set," the detective replied. "We're all armed and besides we've got a sub-machine gun and a supply of tear bombs."

"What do you plan to do?"

Spayne considered the question. "Well," he said, "until I ran into you two while I was sort of scouting the territory, we were thinking of moving right in on them. But I don't know now, with this lady along."

"Go ahead and don't worry about me. I'll stick till the end," Nan said.

"Wait a minute, Spayne," Ben said. "Let me get this straight. You say there are five of you. You've got a machine gun—"

"Right. A Thompson sub."

"And tear bombs?"

"There were about ten in the car and we brought 'em all along when we came on foot the last part of the way."

"Good. Now listen to this plan. I know these Haitians. I know how they react in a fight. These guards are all *cacos* from the hills. They'll fight like demons in a hand to hand encounter, but they're scared stiff of a machine gun. Follow me?"

"Go on," Spayne urged quietly.

"As soon as it's light enough so we can see pretty well, turn that machine gun on. All the guards who are on the grounds will run for the house. They like to get to cover when they hear the bullets whistle.

"Then we'll cover the place and rout them all out with the tear bombs. Capture them without bloodshed."

Spayne was silent for a minute, thinking over Ben's suggestions.

"No," he said finally, "it won't do."

"What's the matter?" Ben asked.

"That's a big house from what I understand. The tear gas would do no good. Even if we managed to toss a few through the windows, those inside could just duck into a different room."

Ben chuckled. "I'll take care of that," he said. "I'll guarantee to rout all the beggars out like rats running from a sinking ship. All I want is one of your men to help me carry the bombs and cover the back side of the house afterwards."

"What's your scheme?" Spayne asked.

"I can't explain it all now, because we've got to get started before it gets light. But we're going in the house. Come on!"

"All right," the detective agreed reluctantly. "If you know what you're doing, I'll take a chance. Follow me and we'll join the rest of the party."

A few minutes later and Spayne was explaining to the four detectives, standing in the shadow of the lodge house, what was up.

"Rourke, you'd better go with Mr. McCray," he said. "Any of you got an extra gun?"

One of the detectives produced a service pistol, which Spayne took and handed to Ben. "You may need it," he said dryly.

"Ben, are you really going back in that terrible place?" Nan asked, a little catch in her voice.

"I've got to, darling," he whispered to her. "Spayne's stuck with me on this thing, and I've got to do my share. I'm the only one who knows the lay of the inside of the house."

"All ready, Rourke?" he asked.

The sergeant replied that he was, and, their arms loaded with as many of the bombs as they could carry, the two men slipped off into the darkness.

XVII

BEN'S STRATEGY

THE SKY WAS BEGINNING TO GROW LIGHT, although the ground beneath the trees was still in utter darkness, and the two men could make out the silhouette of the roof of the house against the east.

With this as a landmark they moved forward on their perilous undertaking. They passed the side of the house some distance away, and then approached stealthily from the rear, where, Ben had figured out, the cellar window he had forced was situated.

There were no lights visible in the place, but McCray could understand this. The voodoo worshippers had all the windows heavily covered with shades, so no passerby might be stirred to curiosity and interrupt the horrible rites that took place within. But he could visualize the scene inside the building with its weird candle illumination. Zareta and the *bocor* conferring on the plans for the recapture of Nan and himself; the two voodoo leaders gloating over the good fortune that had put Chidzic and Bascom in their clutches.

Either by luck, or because the three guards at the gate, who had been overpowered by the detectives, were in the main outside force, they reached the cellar window without encountering any of the machete men.

Ben wriggled through and a few seconds later Rourke joined him in the dust-filled vegetable room, having first passed down the tear bombs.

"Let me have your flashlight," Ben whispered. "I think we can risk it now and then, if I point it at the floor. At least it's better than stumbling into something in the dark."

They advanced carefully into the second cellar room—the hideous charnel house of the *culte des mortes*.

"This is the kind of a gang we're up against," Ben whispered grimly. He shot the beam of light quickly over the shallow boxes with their bleaching corpses, then to the pile of human bones.

"My God!" Rourke gasped. "What are they?"

"The most murderous fanatics in the world," Ben murmured. "It's the *culte des mortes*, which means in English the cult of the corpses. Those are the remains of some of their victims. They use them in their ceremonies and black magic."

In the furnace room, from which the stairs led to the upper part of the house, Ben stopped.

"We wait here," he said in a low voice. "Might as well put the tear bombs on the floor until we get the signal from Spayne."

Ben snapped the light off. The two men stood silently in the darkness, waiting for it to grow light outside. Above they occasionally heard footsteps, and once or twice the muffled sound of a voice, as one of the occupants of the place passed close to the door at the head of the stairs.

Five minutes, ten minutes they waited. Ben was just beginning to fear that something might have gone amiss with their plans, when there came to his straining ears the rippling bark of a machine gun. He snapped the light on and examined the little pile of tear bombs to be sure they were in readiness. Then he whispered to Rourke.

"Have you got a watch?"

"Sure. With a luminous dial," the detective answered.

"Good. We'll allow five minutes and then shoot."

It seemed like an hour to the two men watching the minute hand crawl along the face of Rourke's timepiece. At last Ben snapped the flashlight on again and whispered sharply:

"All right, Rourke! Let's get busy! And we've got to work fast!"

Their task finished, Ben led the way quickly to the vegetable room again.

"As soon as we get outside, we duck for the underbrush and cover the back part of the house. Get me?" he said briskly. The need for silence had passed.

"Sure. You're the chief. I follow you," Rourke replied.

McCray pulled himself up through the narrow cellar window. A little later Rourke joined him. Crouching low, the two men dashed into the bushes.

"This'll do," Ben said. They were standing beside a large tree, in front of which a low mass of shrubbery afforded an excellent screen, at the same time permitting them a view of the back and one side of the house. "We ought to get some action pretty quick."

As if in answer to his words, a window on the first floor at the back of the house was thrown up and a black head appeared. Ben's pistol cracked and a bullet spattered against the sill.

"We've got to prevent that," he said. Then shouted at the top of his lungs: "We'll shoot anyone who shows at a window. Go out the front way and surrender!"

Spayne, apparently, was having a similar experience. From the other side of the grounds came a report, and they could hear the detective lieutenant bellow out a command to the inmates of the house to emerge with their hands up.

They waited a few minutes, but the voodoo worshippers evidently had had enough of opening windows.

"Come on," Ben said. "We'll move over where we can see the other side of the house. I think there's a rear entrance there. Some of them may come out that way."

Rourke close behind, he made his way through the tangle of brush. His conjecture about the rear entrance proved correct and as they caught sight of it, the door opened and a man appeared coughing violently. His hands were hoisted toward the sky.

"Stand where you are!" Ben commanded.

The fellow stopped in his tracks. McCray and Rourke could see he was holding his eyes tightly closed. A few seconds later another figure emerged, a shriveled stooping figure, and Ben laughed grimly.

"That's the buzzard I want," he muttered.

It was the aged *bocor*. He was spluttering and holding a handkerchief to his face, and McCray let the old fellow keep his hands where they were.

No one else came out the back way, although from the front of the house were heard sharp orders from Spayne and the other detectives, which indicated that the voodoo members were pouring into the front yard in numbers.

"I guess these two are all we bag," Ben said finally. "We might as well join the boys in front."

They moved out from the bushes and led their captives along the side of the house to the front.

In the open space beyond the gallery they saw a crowd of the blacks herded together. There were both men and women, and towering above the others, Ben noticed eight or ten of the machete men. While one of the detectives covered them with the machine gun, two others were searching the thoroughly cowed and watery-eyed voodoo members for weapons. Nan was standing at one side with Spayne, who had Chidzic and Bascom in custody.

Ben and Rourke added their two prisoners to the rest, and joined the detective lieutenant.

"You certainly fumigated that pest house," Spayne said to Ben with a grin. "How did you work it?"

Ben laughed. "On my first trip through the cellar I had to go through the furnace room to get upstairs. I happened to notice the heating plant. It was an old-fashioned affair with big pipes leading to open registers in every room. You know the kind.

"After you had fired the machine gun, scaring the guards into the house so they couldn't be sneaking up behind you, Rourke and I let off the tear bombs in the furnace. It was almost made to order; the gas was distributed to every corner of the place."

Spayne appeared puzzled. "But I don't see yet," he said. "The fire-box is cut off from the entrances to the pipes."

"That's right," Ben agreed. "But there's a small door that opens into the heat chamber from the outside. The pipes into the heat chamber, above the fire-box, are open. You see I know all about those old-fashioned furnaces. I used to feed the family coal-eater when I was a boy," he added with a chuckle.

"As soon as we'd chucked the tear grenades in, I opened the air draft which comes in from outdoors, and the gas was sent to every register."

Spayne shook his head. "That's what I get for being born in a big city. The janitor always fired our furnace. And you can't send gas through a steam radiator, anyway."

"Do you think we've got all those vermin out?" he added.

Ben ran his eye over the group of prisoners. "I guessed there must be about forty or fifty, all told. Looks like you've got about that many. Wait!"

He looked carefully at the crowd of blacks again. Then he turned quickly to Spayne.

"Where's Zareta? She's the main one, and I don't see her."

At that moment he noticed that most of the voodoo worshippers had turned their faces up and were staring as well as their gas-affected eyes would permit at the roof of the *houmfort*.

Ben, too, looked up.

He saw the figure of a woman standing on the peak. Her white robe, a great splotch of red across the left breast, fluttered in the breeze; her arms were thrown wide, as though in supplication, toward the morning sun, which was just breaking above the horizon.

"She must have gone out the cupola window," he muttered, and turned to Spayne, who was gazing in fascination at the slender swaying form.

"Quick! After her!" Ben shouted, and seized Spayne's arm.

Even as he spoke, Zareta, priestess of murder and dancer of death, broke into a wild unearthly chant. In it was all the hate, the savagery, yes, even the love, of a thousand jungle ancestors. It seemed to stop the heart beats of those listening below, and to send icy chills racing madly up and down their spines.

She broke off as suddenly as she had started. Then they saw her hand go to her lips; her head bent backwards. Nan stifled a cry and buried her face in her hands.

Zareta, arms still outstretched, fell forward. Over and over she rolled, down the steep roof. Then she shot past the cornice and fell the three stories to the gallery.

Ben was the first to reach her. He found her magnificent body crumpled into a grotesque distortion of one of her famous dancing postures. The green eyes were closed. He knew she was dead, even before he knelt and felt her pulse, because he saw in her hand a tiny phial—manchineel sap!

Then he noticed that the splotch of red on her breast was not, as he had at first imagined, blood. It was an irregular piece of coarse crimson cloth.

He recalled she had also worn it on the Nile green gown at the Grotto. And suddenly he understood.

XVIII

WHY CARTER WAS KILLED

TWO DAYS LATER, MCCRAY LOOKED UP FROM THE DESK in his private office to see the grinning face of Detective Lieutenant Spayne. The latter had every appearance of feeling well pleased with himself.

"Well, I just did it!" he exclaimed, pulling forward a chair and sitting down.

"What did you just do?" Ben laughed. "If you were a cat, I'd judge from your expression that you'd just licked a saucer of cream."

"I made one of our gunmen open up and spill the whole story," the detective announced.

"You mean Chidzic's confessed?"

"Nope. Bascom," Spayne corrected him. "Just kept his hop away from him a while an' he finally broke down and sang the whole song. Couldn't hardly get him to stop when he got started."

Ben nodded his admiration. "Good work. I'd have said you could never get them to talk."

"He did though, and it cleared up lots of things. How Miss Collette got mixed up in this affair for one thing. By the way, how is she?"

"Fine, thanks," Ben said. "Naturally, she was pretty well worn out. But she rested all day yesterday. I'm having dinner with her tonight."

"She's a fine girl," Spayne said. "But, of course, I don't have to tell you that. I never saw a woman go through all she did and not break down completely."

"How about this confession of Bascom's?" Ben asked.

"Well, it'll send 'em both to the hot seat at Sing Sing, all right. Kind of even things up for poor Tom Illick and the other two."

He accepted a cigar, which Ben offered from an opened box, and, when it was nicely lighted, continued.

"It seems this guy Carter hailed originally from Chicago and the redheaded dame who was killed by the fire truck—Chicago Lil—was his sweetheart. Get the situation?"

Ben nodded.

"Carter cleans up in his racketeering out west and decided to move to New York. He quits all his old gang, including Chicago Lil. But she's plumb nuts about him. Still she can't do anything about it at first, because she don't know where he's gone. Then she learns Carter's here.

"She writes him and telegraphs him. It don't do no good. He's off her and makes it plain to her. Then she gets mad. She hops down east. Besides a big bankroll, she's got a letter introducing her to Chidzic as a gent who doesn't mind bumping off a citizen for a price.

"She offers Chidzic ten grand to kill Carter. He agrees and brings in Bascom and a guy named Concelli, who we picked up today. None of 'em know Carter from old man Adam. So Bascom and Concelli goes to the Grotto to find out what he looks like. Eddie figures he's too well known to show his face up there just before a killing's due."

Spayne puffed a moment on his cigar, and then went on with his story.

"But just like a dame, this Chicago Lil has a change of heart. She wants to give this Carter one more chance to take her back. So she phones Chidzic that she's going up to the Grotto. If she leaves with Carter, that means she's patched things up and to lay off him. If not, he's turned her down again, and to kill him.

"Chidzic sends a note to his two mugs, Bascom and Concelli, tipping them off to the new angle. That's the note Zareta found after they accidentally dropped it on the floor."

Ben was thoughtfully blowing the smoke from his cigar into the air.

"And then," he said slowly, "Fate, in the form of a fire truck stepped in. Chicago Lil was killed on the way to the Grotto, I assume. But Nan danced with Carter—and Nan happened to have red hair. Thereby hangs the story. Am I right?"

Spayne nodded. "That's it, I guess."

"To complete the picture from my own experiences," Ben continued, "Zareta found the note and tried to warn Carter. But he wouldn't pay any attention to her. She was madly in love with him, even though he'd cast her off, and after he was killed she determined to revenge his death.

"Naturally, she assumed Nan was the redhead mentioned in the note. So her first step was to get Nan in her power. The next was to prevent me from interfering, if possible. Hence the negro with the poison."

"Sure," Spayne agreed, "and she had all this gang of voodoo worshippers under her, since she was the big gazabo—"

"*Nebo*," Ben corrected him with a chuckle.

"At any rate," Spayne said, "she had a mean gang, and I'm still expecting to have to dig some of them out of their holes. The bunch we grabbed up in Westchester is only a small part."

Ben stood up and glanced at his watch. "Going north?" he asked. "I have to meet Miss Collette in half an hour and I'll drive you up. If you're headed my way."

"No thanks," the detective replied, "I'm staying down here."

Ben took Spayne's hand in a firm grip. "I'm surely grateful for all you did for me."

"Forget it," Spayne muttered with embarrassment. "I had to square things up for Tom Illick, too."

Ben arrived at Nan's apartment promptly on time. He was glad to note that she showed no ill effects from her harrowing experience, beyond a faint shadow under her eyes.

It was still early for them to go out for dinner. In the interval he told her of Spayne's visit and the confession the detective had wrung from Bascom.

"So you see, Nan dear," he said gravely, "it's dangerous to have red hair. Dangerous for other people—especially of the male sex—and sometimes dangerous for yourself."

She laughed. "Seriously, Ben," she said, "there's one thing I want you to explain to me. You remember that red patch Zareta had sewn on her gown at the Grotto?" He nodded, and she continued. "Well, didn't she have another one like it on that robe she wore when she took the poison on the roof of that horrible house?"

"That's right, Nan," Ben said. "You recall what I told you about all these *ouangas*—charms—that are part of the voodoo belief?"

She nodded. "I certainly do. The crossed matches, for a warning to you. And the little bags you found on the one black and in the locker."

"Yes," he replied. "Well, they also have love-*ouangas*. And in order to make them effective, the person trying to work the charm often decorates his clothes with odd and bright patches. I've seen some queer ones in Haiti."

"But why did Zareta wear a charm-patch, if that's what they should be called?"

"Because she had lost Carter's affection and was trying to win it back by means of a love-charm, when he was killed. She undoubtedly had similar patches on all her clothes," Ben explained.

"And it failed to work," Nan said half-sadly.

"Yes, it failed. It failed just the way the hate-*ouangas* failed, and the warning to me."

She looked at him somberly, but he thought he detected a faint twitching at the corner of her mouth as she spoke.

"Then you don't believe in charms?"

"Oh, sure I do!" Ben exclaimed. "I believe in a certain kind of charms."

"What kind are they?" she asked. As he folded her in his arms, Nan knew the answer, but, womanlike, she waited eagerly to hear it.

"Your kind of charms, Nan dearest!"

The Line-Up
(excerpt)

Where readers meet at DETECTIVE-DRAGNET *Headquarters to inspect the stories as they pass under the critical Spotlight of other readers.*

Supervised by INSPECTOR JOHNSON

HELLO, SLEUTHS.

. . .

Now we'll start off the *Line-Up*. The first fellow you see up there on the platform is Maxwell Hawkins who wrote the "Cult of the Corpses" in this issue. Hawkins has a few words to say on voodoo worshippers.

Let's go, Hawkins.

Hello Inspector:

Although the subject of voodooism—that mysterious and sinister corruption of ancient jungle beliefs in combination with certain naive interpretations by the black men of the teachings of Christianity—first attracted my attention more than thirteen years ago; it was not until recently that two almost trivial incidents in New York City turned my mind back along familiar tracks of thought and started me writing "The Cult of the Corpses."

The mystical and occult, especially when associated with barbaric and inhuman practices, is heavily charged with interest for the curious minded, and I plead guilty to a plentiful supply of noisiness. And so it was that when I joined the Navy at the entrance of this country into the World War, and some of the old timers among the gobs, and one or two leathernecks I became acquainted with, began to spin yarns about the voodoo worshippers of Haiti, I was all ears. Then and there was born a resolution to find out about some of these weird rites that took place in the jungles of the mysterious island at first hand.

But having accomplished this, and made more or less of a study of the subject, I gradually let the matter slide from my mind until about six months ago.

I was talking one day to the janitor of the apartment house in which I was then living. He was a colored man, a native of Haiti and, so he had told me, a graduate of one of the missionary colleges.

"Grant," I said, "what do you know about voodooism?"

His eyes opened wide and he hesitated a long time before replying.

"Mr. Hawkins," he said at last, "I know more about it than any of you white folks would believe."

With a little prodding, he narrated experiences that had taken place during his boyhood as a ragged, barefooted native in the hinterland of Haiti. I had never been able to verify the existence of *zombies* to my own satisfaction, preferring to accept the explanation that these half-life slaves were victims of a pernicious drug, if they existed at all. But Grant was particularly emphatic in proclaiming that they not only existed, but that he had seen them working in the fields many times.

Then it occurred to me that although you might take the voodoo worshippers out of Haiti, to paraphrase an old saying, you couldn't take the voodooism out of the Haitians.

About two months later, this was brought home to me more forcibly.

I was sitting in a Harlem night club. My eye lighted on the trap drummer. He was beating his large kettle drum with the heel of his hand, and the sound was oddly akin to the spine-prickling boom of the *rada* drums of the Haitian jungle. The story of "The Cult of the Corpses" began to take shape in my mind at that moment—the transplanting of the most horrible of the offshoots of voodooism—the *Culte des Mortes*—from the jungles which nature had built on a tropical island to the jungles of brick and stone, which man had built on another island, Manhattan, far to the north.

"The Cult of the Corpses" began in a night club. So it was only natural that when I set it on paper—I began it in a night club!

MAXWELL HAWKINS.

Letherius pushed Peggy toward the
gaping mouth of the machine.

Dealers in Death

To the skyscraper canyons of New York came Mr. Letherius, a weird man who had made exhaustive researches—in the art of murder! For thirteen long years he had delved into the murders down through the centuries—and developed two hundred detection-proof methods of killing mankind. . . . And the most fiendish of them all, he had planned for the beautiful Peggy Delcarn!

I

MR. LETHERIUS

THE PORTLY GRAY-HAIRED MAN, with the gardenia tucked into the lapel of his coat, leaned forward.

"Well, what shall I tell him the price is?" he asked.

The other man in the luxuriously furnished room, to whom the question was addressed, dropped long, black lashes over his eyes. He let his head loll backward as if to rest. But a reddish glint from between those silken, almost feminine eyelashes that lay on his ashen cheeks betrayed that he was still watching.

There was a silence. The man with the corpse-like face seemed not to breathe. He might well have been mistaken for a dead man, except for a slow movement of the little finger of his right hand on the arm of the chair. Up and down it went in rhythmic count.

A slight frown creased his high pallid brow. Suddenly he stood up without a word and crossed the room. His figure was of medium height, frail and slightly bent, like a student who has pored too long over his books. As he walked, his steps were muffled by the deep rug.

Pushing aside a heavy tapestry, he touched the wall. At once, a section the size of a door slid back and he passed through.

The man wearing the gardenia, as though used to such actions as he had just witnessed, shrugged faintly. He reached into his pocket and brought forth a cigar. When he had it well lighted, he settled back in his chair to wait.

About him was an air of prosperity and easy assurance. He was immaculately dressed in an expensively tailored dark suit, and his hands, holding limp gloves, rested on the curve of a Malacca walking stick.

While he sat patiently, blowing the fragrant Havana smoke through his full lips, he raised his fingers from time to time to dab at the waxed ends of his mustache. His eyes, pale gray with pink lids, roamed the room.

The heavy drapes, the dark carved furniture, and the many exotic *objets d'art* seemingly awakened little interest in him. He was like a fat poodle awaiting the whim of his master.

Presently the thin, stooping figure of the other appeared.

"It's just as I was afraid, Bonwix," he said.

"How's that?" the man with the gardenia asked.

"I have no records on the girl. That department of our undertaking has not been fully developed, although we are working on it. All our cases to date have been men."

"Well, what shall I tell him? What price? I promised him I'd come back and let him know this afternoon," Bonwix said.

The man with the ashen face resumed his seat without answering. He touched the tips of his fingers lightly together. Once more he closed his eyes and leaned back in that deceptive attitude of near coma. At last he spoke, softly and with a purr in his tone.

"I'll have to make him an offhand price on what you have outlined to me. You may tell Mr. Delcarn"—he hesitated for a second—"that for thirty-thousand dollars, we shall be very pleased to murder his niece!" His lips tightened in a sardonic smile.

Bonwix appeared dubious. "It seems like a pretty high figure."

"You can assure him that ours will be a thoroughly high class job. And he can rest secure in the knowledge that not the faintest hint of suspicion will fall upon him."

"But we have done them for much less and—"

Bonwix broke off and half-shrank in his chair. The other's black eyes glowed redly, a danger signal the man with the gardenia recognized.

"Certainly we have done them more cheaply! Six months ago when you and I began this enterprise we received a paltry five-thousand dollars from our first client. But times have changed. For removing Judge Wilmerfield from the cares of this world, we received fifty-thousand dollars."

His face relaxed and two tiny flushed spots that had appeared in his cheeks faded, leaving them their usual gravel-like hue.

"You forget," he continued quietly, "that before I took you in with me as my business agent, I had practiced alone in an experimental fashion. You forget, also, that for thirteen years I prepared myself to take up murder as a profession. I have developed more than two hundred detection-proof methods of committing homicide. I have bent for hours over volumes dealing with the crime down through the centuries. I have—"

He changed the subject with a wave of his tapering hand.

"But I have told you all that before. The point I wish to make—and I trust you mark it well," he added significantly, "is that I—I, Letherius, am in charge. My word shall not be questioned. My commands shall be obeyed!"

"I understand," Bonwix mumbled relaxing.

"To get back to Mr. Delcarn and his niece," Letherius resumed calmly. "I fixed my price, of course, on what you told me. But knowing your natural conservativeness, I imagine he will benefit much more than you realize by her death. On second thought, therefore, you will kindly quote him a figure of forty-thousand dollars.

"One minute!" he cautioned as Bonwix started to speak.

Letherius moved to a massive desk at one side of the room and pressed a button. Then he took his chair again.

"We may as well get started," he said. "Preparedness is one of the first rules of success in this business. That's where all the other paid killers, especially the gangster-gunman type, have always failed. Until I entered the field, everything was done in haphazard fashion. No one seemed to realize that it could be made into a scientific enterprise, operated on a large scale and highly profitable."

"Oh, it's paid all right," Bonwix agreed.

"Paid! A half-million dollars in six months is not to be laughed at for an infant industry," Letherius replied with a grim chuckle. "And, my dear Bonwix, we have merely scraped the surface. I have often meditated on the possibility of murdering those persons who wish to commit suicide, yet lack the moral courage to take their own lives. Now for a fee—"

He was interrupted by a knock on the door and in response to a word from him, two young men entered. They approached Letherius and stood deferentially, almost with an air of awe.

"If I may trouble you to write down the name of our new client and his—ah—prospect. Mortboy, will you kindly get cards and pen for Mr. Bonwix," he added.

One of the young men brought two white cards and a fountain pen from the desk and Bonwix took them in his plump hand.

"You might add a word of description," Letherius suggested.

"I've never seen the girl," the other replied, finishing his writing and handing over the cards.

One of them Letherius gave to the young man he had addressed as Mortboy. He glanced at the remaining card and passed it to the other young man.

"You have the girl, Jenks," he said. "That is the more important assignment, because we have no data on her. Find out about her past, her habits, her friends—the usual procedure. You, Mortboy, do the same with the man. We must bring our record on him up to date. That's all."

As Mortboy and Jenks nodded and left the room, Bonwix rose.

"I suppose I may as well be on my way," he said. "I'll go right to Delcarn's office and give him our price."

Picking up his bowler hat, he started toward the door with a shake of his head. A sudden macabre laugh made him swing in alarm.

Letherius was leaning back in his chair, his pasty face contorted with amusement.

"What—what's the matter?" exclaimed Bonwix.

"You—you, my dear Bonwix," replied Letherius, controlling himself. He became suddenly serious. "For six months you have been my business agent—my contact man—yet you have never thought of the most beautiful aspect of our occupation."

Bonwix was annoyed, but he steadied himself. "I don't understand."

"You were thinking as you started to leave, 'I'll bet Delcarn won't come across with that much money for this job.' Tell me, weren't you?"

"Well, as a matter of fact, I was," the other admitted grudgingly.

Letherius stood up. Beside the fat Bonwix he made a startling contrast. One was carefully clad, the other with carelessness. One was to all appearances a prosperous business man and the other an underfed clerk. Yet such was the dynamic quality of Letherius that there could be no doubt which was master and which was man.

"Get this!" Letherius whipped out acidly. "We do not have to haggle with our clients. When they come to us, we name our price. They *always* accept it!"

"What do you mean?"

"You will kindly make it clear to Mr. Delcarn that if he does not wish to pay us forty-thousand dollars to take the life of his niece, it is going to be our pleasure to murder him without cost."

II

A SHADOW FALLS

THUD! SMACK!

"Come on now! One-two! Use your right! Holy smoke, ain't you got no right? Attababy!"

Thud! Thud! Smack!

The sound of leather meeting leather or flesh filled the low-ceilinged room above the garage. Back and forth, punching, jabbing, went the two men, darting in and out with the lithe activeness of cats.

"That's enough for today!" one of them suddenly exclaimed.

They both sat down breathing strongly on a bench against the wall.

"Well, Batt, am I getting any better?"

The man addressed as Batt, a well-built individual in his forties with a slightly flattened nose, looked at the speaker with unconcealed admiration.

"Better? Say, I'm tellin' you, Mr. Trask, with a year of work I could make you a champ, even if you are pretty old to be startin' in the fight game. It's too bad you got all that dough and don't have to earn your way," he added, almost mournfully.

Theodore Trask laughed. "I'm afraid you overestimate me."

"Not me," replied Batt emphatically. "I was in the ring ten years. I know a fighter with heart when I see him. And look how you shape up! Then, too, you was a runner in college. That makes your footwork awful fast."

"I'm sorry the fighting profession will have to struggle along without me," Ted Trask grinned. "I like boxing, though. Maybe that influenced me in hiring you as my chauffeur."

"You sure treated me white," Batt said, "picking me up like—"

"Forget it!" interrupted Ted, embarrassed.

"I'll never forget it. Say, I was right at bottom that night I braced you for the price of a cup of java. 'Bout ready to take the count that don't end. You took me in, fed me and before I knew it I was respectable again with a swell job." There was a hint of moisture in the old battler's eyes.

Ted changed the subject. "How did it happen you were never champion, Batt?" he asked.

"Not quite good enough. I fought the champ and stayed with him eight rounds. But in the ninth—" The veteran of the squared circle made a grimace. "Honest, I thought they'd dropped the roof on me."

"Too bad," Ted said sympathetically. "But it's something to have fought the champ for the title."

He got up suddenly. "I'd better be trotting back to the house and dressing. I have to go to town this afternoon."

"Will you want me to drive you?"

"No, I'll drive myself in the roadster."

They walked together down the stairs that led to the lower part of the garage. Batt watched Ted's six-foot figure swing along the short walk to the house.

"So he wants to drive hisself," the chauffeur chuckled softly. "Don't want no one sittin' in front, catchin' a word now and then maybe." He clucked between his teeth. "There's going to be a missus around these trainin' quarters before long, and I'll bet I know who it is."

Upstairs in the rambling white house, which faced Long Island Sound, Ted took a thorough if hurried shower and presently was dressing with what might have seemed unnecessary care. But at twenty-six a man is apt to take special pains with his attire—when going into New York to keep a very important engagement with a very beautiful girl.

He glanced at his wrist watch and gave a low whistle.

"Better hurry," he said to himself. "Peggy'll bite my ear off if I'm late!" He laughed aloud. The idea of brown-eyed little Peggy biting his ear amused him. If that happy bit of mayhem were possible, he decided, he would make a point of being late.

Behind the wheel of his motorcar he pushed his foot down and the low, green speedster shot out of the driveway and onto the road which led to the main highway. What Ted referred to casually as "the roadster" was a glistening streak of lightning on wheels. The makers guaranteed it would do a hundred and thirty-five. Ted had put it up to a hundred and twenty-eight on the speedway and taken the salesman's word for the other seven miles an hour.

In no time at all he was in Great Neck—Little Neck—Bayside.

Across the Queens Bridge, and after slipping through the uptown traffic like some mammoth eel, the green car pulled to a stop in front of a graystone house in the east seventies.

The structure, like so many of its neighbors, had been converted into apartments of small size. Ted entered the vestibule and pressed a button beneath the card bearing the name Delcarn.

"Gee, Peggy, it's great to see you again!" he exclaimed, taking both her hands as soon as they were inside her little apartment.

"You sound as if we hadn't been together for ages," Peggy Delcarn replied, smiling. "Why it's been only—"

"Oh, well, it seemed like ages to me," Ted broke in. "How goes the vacation?"

Peggy sighed. "Only four more days. Then Miss Peggy Delcarn again becomes the efficient business woman."

"If you'd only listen to me, dear," Ted said frowning, "you know how many times—"

"Six!" laughed Peggy. "I always keep very accurate account of my proposals. To a girl they're just as important as scalps to an Indian brave."

She sat down on a low divan—by night, with its many cushions removed, it automatically became a bed. Ted sat beside her. His manner became grave.

"Do you really mean you are going to stick to that ridiculous idea—you won't marry me until I go into business—get a job?"

"Yes." The brown eyes with their frame of curling lashes were serious. There was a determined set to the red lips, surprising in lips that looked so soft and yielding.

"But why should I work?" Ted protested.

"Well, for one thing, when I get married I don't want a husband around cluttering up the place while I'm doing the housework during the day."

"Housework!" Ted's tone was one of utter amazement. There flashed into his mind a picture of the rambling white house out on Long Island. He never had been sure whether there were three maids and two housemen or three housemen and two maids. Not to mention Batt, a gardener, and a laundress.

"But, dear, if you marry me, you won't have to do housework!"

"Oh, but I will!" Peggy bobbed her head emphatically. The movement brought out the golden tints in her waving chestnut hair. "When I get married, I want to try out this love in a cottage—at least for a few years," she added with feminine caution. "I'm going to be right at the door in a gingham apron every night to greet *my man* when he comes home from work."

Ted looked glum. Suddenly she turned to him and she was smiling.

"Come on, Ted. We're both stubborn, but I don't want to let that spoil my vacation. It was bad enough to have to spend it in the city."

"That's right, Peggy. Sorry I was thoughtless." He stood up. "What do you want to do? How about running out with me to a roadhouse on the Merrick Road I know of and having a shore dinner. We can dance there," he said as an added inducement.

"Great!" she exclaimed. "I'll be with you in a jiffy."

She disappeared into the only other room the apartment boasted of and a minute later emerged with a rakish little tricorn hat on. In her hands she held gloves and a light coat, which Ted took from her, while she put on the gloves. Her expression was thoughtful.

"There's only one thing—"

"What's that?"

"I promised Uncle Giles I'd drop in at his office this afternoon. He phoned that he had something important to tell me. He's a funny old fellow, but he's the only relative I have in the world and I'm really awfully fond of him. Blood's thicker than water, I guess," she added with a wistful smile.

"Oh, that's all right," Ted said, looking at his watch. "You'll have plenty of time. I'll take you. Where's his office?"

"Down in the financial district on William Street," she answered.

He held the door open for her and they started down the stairs. Peggy's firm grip on his arm sent a warm glow all over him.

"I'm glad you're with me," she nodded. "I want you to meet Uncle Giles and I want him to meet you."

When they reached the sidewalk, Peggy started for the green roadster, but Ted turned her up the street.

"We can hail a taxi at the corner," he said with a grin. Then explaining, as he noted with amusement her puzzled expression, "I'm not going to have all the traffic between here and William Street diverting my attention. I want to be able to concentrate on you."

"Aren't you afraid someone will steal it?"

"Not much chance. It's got exceptionally good locks both on the gears and the ignition," Ted replied. He raised his hand and a cab drew to the curb with screeching brakes.

The office building before which the taxi halted at Peggy's direction was one that had been built a number of years before. It now seemed almost shabby and small beside its towering fellows, although only fifteen years had passed since it had been pointed to with pride.

"It's on the tenth floor," Peggy said as they entered.

They had a brief wait for an elevator car and then started up.

"What did your uncle say he wanted to see you for?" Ted asked on the way.

"I haven't any idea. He just said it was important. It's so seldom he asks me to do anything that I agreed right away to come down here. I was a little curious, too," she admitted.

They walked along the corridor of the tenth floor toward the rear of the building. The faint click of typewriters and the hum of conversation came from behind some of the many doors; others were dark and silent and Ted surmised that the building was far from being fully rented.

"There it is—the last one," Peggy said pointing.

When they were about ten feet away the door suddenly opened. A man came out, closed it, and turned abruptly to stride off. As he did so he collided violently with Ted. The impact almost threw the stranger off his feet. But he recovered and was profuse in his apologies, bowing repeatedly.

"Don't mention it," Ted said. "It was mostly my fault. I wasn't watching."

Tipping his bowler hat, the other man continued on his way.

"Quite a dressy gentleman with his gardenia and Malacca stick," Peggy remarked.

"He had funny eyes, did you notice?" Ted asked.

"No."

"I think they were gray, but they had pink lids. Not very pleasant looking."

Peggy put her hand on the knob of the door from which the man with the gardenia had just emerged.

"Here we are."

She opened the door and Ted followed her into the office. It was, so far as he could see at first glance, composed of a single room. A window looked out upon a dark areaway and the gray light which came through it was increased by a lone electric light bulb hanging on a long cord from the ceiling.

At the window, his hands clasped behind him, stood a man, a short rather broad-shouldered man. Ted's first impression of him was that he was entirely baldheaded. As he wheeled at the noise of their entrance, however, Ted saw that two gray tufts extended out above each ear.

"Ah, it's you, my dear little Peggy," he said and came forward to take her hand and pat her on the back.

She introduced him to Ted. "This is Uncle Giles."

Ted found himself seizing a cold, soft hand and mumbling a word of acknowledgment. He almost towered above the other man, who was not much taller than Peggy. With an effort, Ted restrained a laugh as he looked down at the moon-face of Delcarn, smooth shaven and slightly pop-eyed. It was a face that seemed so remote from the man's name—it was absolutely guileless, Ted fancied.

"Well, well, I'm glad you came down to see your old uncle," Delcarn was saying to Peggy. "But, I'm sure you won't regret it when you find out the nice surprise I have for you. And I'm so glad to meet your friend Mr.—Mr.—"

"Trask," Ted supplied.

"Yes, Mr. Trask. In fact, that's quite fortunate. He can be of assistance. But sit down. I'm forgetting my duties as host to a charming niece."

Delcarn brought forward two straight-backed chairs and placed them facing a scarred flattop desk, behind which he seated himself. When Peggy and Ted had made themselves as comfortable as their chairs would permit, he offered Ted a cigar.

"Thanks, but I'll smoke a cigarette, if you don't mind," the younger man said.

"Not at all. And how have you been, my dear?" Delcarn said, turning his mild eyes on his niece.

"On my vacation and in the best of health as a result," Peggy replied with a laugh. "And you?"

Giles Delcarn gave a little sigh. "As well as could be expected. But at my age one doesn't expect perfect health."

"At your age?" Peggy repeated in surprise. "Why, Uncle Giles you can't be a day more than fifty-eight."

"Sixty," he corrected. "But that reminds me of the reason I asked you to come down here, and I dare say you are anxious to get away from an old fellow like me and out with this young gentleman."

She started to protest, but Delcarn raised his hand. First he looked at Peggy and then at Ted, after which he cleared his throat with an attempt at impressiveness.

"My dear, I wanted you to come to my office because I have just made a new will."

Ted saw Peggy's brown eyes widen. Her uncle was looking fixedly at the desktop now.

"Yes, my dear," he continued, "I have made it—a half-hour ago to be exact—and I have left everything to you. Everything!"

Peggy was stunned, Ted was sure. She started to speak and then got up and went to Delcarn and put her arm on his shoulder.

"But—but—uncle, you shouldn't have done that. It's simply sweet of you, of course, but—"

"Who else should I leave my money to?" he asked sharply.

"Why—oh, charities—"

"Bah!" the little round-faced man said with an almost comical violence. "But I wanted to tell you about it, because, my dear, in an earlier will I disposed of most of my estate in an entirely different fashion. In the event of my death, I wanted you to know of the existence of this later instrument."

Peggy was quite overcome, speechless with surprise and gratitude. But her uncle waved her away.

"Now that you are here with your friend, he can be one of the witnesses, if he will be so kind?"

"Glad to," Ted said.

"If you'll excuse me for a few minutes, I'll go to the public stenographer's office. It's right on this floor. The young woman in there is typing the document and she can be the other witness."

Delcarn disappeared out the door. Peggy looked at Ted and he saw that she still seemed stunned by what had just happened.

"Surprised you, didn't he?" Ted grinned. "Has he got much money?"

"Honestly, Ted, I don't know. I think he has quite a lot. He's always been so—well, if he wasn't my uncle I'd say he was a darn old miser, even if he doesn't look the part."

"You mean to say he's never helped you out?"

"Not a red cent. Not that I ever wanted him to," Peggy hastened to add, "but—" She broke off at the sound of a step outside.

The door opened and Delcarn entered, holding a couple of sheets of paper in his hand.

"Here it is," he said, handing one copy to Peggy and the other to Ted. "Everything ship-shape."

It was a short will, three paragraphs long, Ted saw, and, after the customary provision for paying any outstanding debts against the deceased, left his entire estate to Margaret Elizabeth Delcarn.

"Where do I sign?" the younger man asked.

"Come sit here and I'll show you," Delcarn said, drawing out the chair at the desk.

When both copies had been duly witnessed by Ted, Peggy's uncle folded them carefully and took them to a small, old-fashioned safe in one corner of the office. The door already was unlocked and he swung it quickly back. As he did so, two large-sized envelopes dropped to the floor. With what seemed to Ted unnecessary haste, Delcarn stooped to recover them, almost toppling over in his eagerness.

After recovering the envelopes, he placed them with the copies of the will in the safe and closed and locked the door. Then he turned to his two visitors.

"Run along now, you two children, and enjoy yourselves," he said, almost crustily.

Peggy went up to him and kissed him lightly on the cheek. "You don't know, Uncle Giles, how much this affects me," she said. "I never expected anything like it. I don't know exactly what to say to thank you."

Ted fancied Delcarn's face paled. His manner, however, was petulant and embarrassed.

"Let's not say any more about it," he mumbled. "Now run along!"

At the door, Peggy turned back to him.

"Wouldn't you like to come out to my apartment and have me cook you dinner? You don't know what a marvelous meal I can prepare in my closet-kitchenette."

"Thank you, child, thank you," Delcarn muttered, "but I am going out of town for a few days—perhaps a week. Leaving this afternoon. Good-bye."

When Peggy and Ted were once more on the street, she looked at him quizzically. "Well, what do you think of Uncle Giles?"

"You were right. He's a queer cuss. When we came in he was all honey and molasses, but he almost pushed us out of his office."

"It wasn't quite so bad as that," Peggy laughed. "But he did seem preoccupied. Probably thinking about the trip he said he was going on."

"Here's a cab!" exclaimed Ted, as an alert driver spotted them and drew to the curb. "Let's get started for Long Island."

Even while they were getting in, a young man slipped out from the lobby of the building and hailed a second cab. He pressed a bill into the driver's hand. He spoke a few words and nodded almost imperceptibly toward the taxi in which Ted and Peggy were settling back in the seat.

III

THE VOICE OF DEATH

LETHERIUS SAT HUNCHED OVER THE MASSIVE DESK, the frailness of his figure accentuated by its bulk. In contrast to earlier in the day, when he had conferred with Bonwix, his black eyes were wide open. They burned steadily now with that unholy reddish light.

Before him were spread a sheaf of papers, several filing cards, and a number of books. He was studying the papers carefully, his arms extended on the desktop. The little finger of his right hand moved rhythmically up and down, like a tiny pendulum ticking off the seconds until doom.

Although he was devoting his attention to the data before him, from time to time Letherius raised his head as if to listen. When the light fell on his corpse-like face, it showed two flushed spots the size of a dime on his ashen cheeks.

He pressed one of the half-dozen buttons at the side of the desk. A few seconds later, a small brown man with slanting eyes entered soundlessly.

"Have you any word from Mr. Bonwix?"

The Malay shook his head in the negative.

"That's all, Ko. Show him up the minute he arrives."

The servant salaamed and left the room as quietly as he had entered.

Letherius pushed the papers he had been studying to one side and sat up. He fixed his gaze on the wall and remained motionless, only his little finger moving with its clocklike precision.

He was still in the same position, when Ko ushered Bonwix into the room fifteen minutes later. At the entrance of his business agent, however, Letherius arose and advanced to greet him.

"Ah, my dear Bonwix, you did well to come in person. The telephone is all right for ordinary reports, but in a matter of this kind we should not talk over public wires, even if we use the code."

Bonwix planted his heavy hulk in a chair and Letherius continued, he, too, sitting down.

"I do not need to ask you if you have been successful. Your expression speaks for you. You had no trouble?"

"None worth mentioning," the business agent replied. "As I anticipated, he balked a little at the price. I made a pretense of leaving and he came through. It was not necessary to use our threat."

"Good! I always prefer to have these matters closed in a peaceful way. They have been so far," Letherius murmured with a cynical smile curling his lip.

"He is certainly anxious to have this niece of his erased," Bonwix said.

"You didn't, by chance, learn why?"

The business agent shook his head. "I tried to lead him into it, but he side-stepped my questions. He is very crafty."

"And rich," added Letherius. "Of that, I have made certain. But about the reason for this determination to have his niece murdered. That is no concern of ours. We do not want to know why! We receive an order for the work. We execute the order. The transaction is closed. Except—the money!"

The fat man blushed. "Excuse me," he mumbled. Reaching into his inside coat pocket, he brought out a thick package, which he handed to Letherius. "I waited while he went to the bank."

Without unwrapping it, Letherius tossed the money to the desk. "There will be a dividend the end of the month," he said significantly.

He was silent for a short time, while the business agent waited for him to speak.

"There is only one thing I have not yet been able to determine," Letherius said at last.

"What's that?"

"What method to employ in blotting out the girl. With a man it is utterly simple. Men are creatures of habit. You can count with a reasonable degree of certainty on what their next move will be. With a woman"—he waved his hand gracefully—"they are apt to start on a little trip of a mile and change their minds four times on the way."

"Why not use the plan we did on old Wilmerfield?"

Letherius shook his head. "No. That was all right for an old man. An accidental fall. But this is a young and active girl. Of course, there is much to be said for the murder of accident, as I call it. But it must be very carefully staged."

"Why not just a straight out-and-out killing. Let the Strangler work on her. She's an almost unknown working girl and there won't be much row raised over it," Bonwix suggested.

"No, no!" the ashen-faced man muttered with an expression of distaste.

"I prefer to have no violence unless—it is necessary! Then, of course, I will stop at nothing!" His eyes flashed like red danger signals but he at once grew calm again.

"In a city the size of New York," Letherius continued thoughtfully, "a great many girls disappear every month, never to be heard of again. I have meditated on the sudden disappearance method, with the killing and disposal of the body at leisure, but—"

He got up and began to walk slowly back and forth across the room, his head bowed lower than ever, his tapering hands clasped behind him.

Finally he sat at the desk and pressed one of the buttons. Bonwix watched in silence. He knew from experience not to interrupt at such a time. Letherius leaned his ghastly brow on his open palm and did not raise his head until a knock sounded on the door.

"Enter!" he exclaimed, straightening up.

A small man wearing spectacles entered. He wore a white, but badly stained, laboratory apron. His fingers, too, bore many stains. Respectfully he walked to the desk at which Letherius was sitting.

"You wished to speak with me?" the newcomer asked, voicing with a strong accent.

"Yes. Have you continued with the experiments I started you on this morning, Silvitch?"

"Yes, sir. That virus—"

"Which virus?" snapped Letherius impatiently. "Be specific!"

"Of the bubonic plague, sir," the man with the spectacles replied. "It is no good. I am afraid the culture died in coming to this country."

"No matter. We shall get some more. And the other experiments?"

"Number 738-A has worked out to perfection, sir."

"You have tested it? All the tests?"

"Yes, sir."

"What was the time of reaction on white rats?"

"Two-fifths of a second, sir."

"And guinea pigs?"

"Four-fifths of a second."

"You then tried the experiment on them after exposing the substance to the air for an hour, as I directed you?"

"Yes, sir. It was harmless and could not be identified by any ordinary laboratory methods," Silvitch answered.

"Let me congratulate you," Letherius said. "That's all."

The man with the spectacles dipped his head in an awkward bow and retired through the door by which he had entered.

Letherius, an expression of malevolent joy on his repulsive face, leaped to his feet. All signs of languor had dropped from him.

"Bonwix!" His voice seemed to cut through the air. "Did you give Delcarn his instructions about his alibi?"

"I told him to get out of town and to take a reliable witness with him," Bonwix replied. "He is leaving for Detroit at seven o'clock."

Letherius rubbed his hands. "Good. Mortboy will shadow him there." He noted an expression of surprise on the business agent's face.

"My God, man!" exclaimed Letherius impatiently. "Have you been handling the negotiations for this murder company for six months, and still know nothing about our operating methods?"

Bonwix tried to stammer an answer, but Letherius interrupted.

"We must watch our clients as well as our victims. For instance, we might be placed in an embarrassing position if they should become conscience-stricken and decide to stop us after we had started."

"I understand now," the other murmured abashed. "But I've been devoting myself to getting the business and the money. That's enough for one man."

"Quite right," Letherius agreed. "But you may as well know that we shadow our clients for some time after the deal is closed—and the goods are delivered. Some idiot might get remorse, and sic the police on us; then commit suicide or skip the country. It wouldn't do much good," he added darkly.

"How long did you tell Delcarn to stay in Detroit?" he asked abruptly.

"A week."

Letherius suddenly gave vent to one of his blood-chilling macabre laughs.

"Much too long, my dear Bonwix. And you can go home and have pleasant dreams tonight, because—tonight we strike!"

IV

SUSPICIONS

AS THE CAB IN WHICH PEGGY AND TED HAD RIDDEN up from the financial district turned the corner onto the street where she lived, she seized his arm with a quick movement.

"There—it's just as I told you. Your car's gone!"

He followed her glance. The low sleek roadster was no longer in front of the graystone house.

"The police have probably hauled it off for parking too long," Ted suggested.

"That isn't possible," she replied positively. "We've only been gone a couple of hours and there isn't any parking limit on this block. No, it's been stolen. What a shame!"

Ted paid the driver off and they stood indecisively at the curb.

"Well, they won't get very far with it," he said at last. "I don't believe there are half a dozen cars just like it in the whole country, it's so conspicuous. Probably someone took it for a joy-ride. I hope they don't try to open it up," he added thoughtfully.

"Why?"

"They'll get killed—unless they're used to traveling more than a hundred miles an hour. I'll notify the police right away. Anyway, it was insured, honey," he said patting her shoulder.

"There goes our shore dinner," Peggy murmured with pretended tears. "And how I love shore dinners!"

Ted laughed heartily. "This doesn't upset our plans. I'll just phone Batt to bring the closed car in and we'll take a taxi to Queens Plaza and meet him."

"My, don't you do things in the grand manner!" Peggy's tone was bantering, but there was an underlying note of admiration.

"Do you want to get anything in your apartment?" he asked.

"If we go in the closed car, I think I'll change my dress, if you don't mind waiting."

"You run on upstairs," Ted said, "and I'll go down to the corner and telephone Batt. Also, I'll notify the police about the car having been stolen."

She nodded agreement. "Ring the bell four times, and I'll come down. I'm certain I'll be ready before you make your calls."

With a wave, she disappeared into the entryway of the house and Ted walked rapidly down the street to the drugstore on the corner.

He telephoned the police station first, then gave the operator the number of his home on Long Island. As he waited for the suburban call to be made, he glanced idly out of the booth. A man, apparently waiting to use the phone, was standing unnecessarily close to the glass door with his back turned.

"Thinks he's going to get an earful of some fellow talking to a girl," Ted growled to himself. "Well, I hope this amuses him."

Further comment on the man outside was cut off by a voice answering at the other end of the wire. It was one of the maids. Ted quickly gave his orders for Batt to meet him.

"And, Celeste," he added, "tell Aunt Lucy not to fret if I'm out late. We're going to the Wildfire Inn." He hung up with an annoyed click. "Nothing worse than a doting aunt," he grumbled as he swung open the door of the booth.

The man who had seemed so impatient to use the phone booth was leaning over the cigar case, apparently much interested in the boxes of cigars on display. Ted walked up and laid in a supply of cigarettes. The other turned and entered the booth, but Ted caught a good look at a thin, wolfish face.

Four rings on the bell at the graystone house brought an immediate response. Peggy appeared as if by magic, smiling and eager. She had changed to a more formal dress of dark green crepe that set off the delicate curves of her lovely figure.

"By George, you look magnificent!" Ted's voice left no doubt that he meant it.

Peggy flushed with pleasure. "I'm glad you like it. It's new. But it's a little too blowy to wear in an open car."

"Let's go!" Ted exclaimed. "I can hardly wait to lead this green vision onto a dance floor!"

Their taxicab was caught in the evening jam of traffic across the bridge towards Queens and they arrived at the plaza to find Batt there ahead of them.

"How do you do, miss," he said, greeting Peggy with the best he had in the way of smiles. And to Ted, "It's too bad you had the roadster stolen. But the cops'll pick it up pretty quick. It sticks out like a black eye."

"I think so, too," Ted agreed. "We want to go to the Wildfire Inn. Do you know where that is?"

"Yes, sir. On the Merrick Road," Batt answered, closing the car door and climbing behind the wheel.

The big car rolled swiftly over the boulevards. Batt, whose skill as a driver was equal to his skill with the gloves, glided in and out of the stream of vehicles. When they reached the big frame roadhouse with its wide porches it was still daylight, although the sun was just about to dip below the horizon.

"I have an appetite as big as a mountain!" Peggy exclaimed exuberantly as they passed through the door into a hall with a cloak-room off it.

"Here's the place to take care of that," Ted grinned. "Let me check my hat and we'll go in and pick out a table you like."

They had no trouble getting the table Peggy liked. When head-waiters saw Ted they instinctively gave him just what he wanted, or his companion wanted.

"How do you like the place?" he asked as soon as they had given their orders.

Peggy looked around. The main room was taken up mostly by the dance floor. A six-piece orchestra was resting between numbers in the far corner. The broad verandahs contained most of the tables for the diners and these were about half occupied. The roadhouse was decorated with taste and moderation, entirely lacking in the crude garishness of the city night clubs.

"I think it's splendid!" Peggy exclaimed.

Ted was pleased at her enthusiasm. "It gets a little more lively later on. There goes the music! Let's dance a few steps before our food comes."

When they returned from the dance floor, their first course was ready for them.

The food was excellent and for a while they devoted themselves to it, with snatches of conversation between bites. But as the waiter brought their coffee, Ted looked at Peggy with a twinkle in his eye.

"Well, how does it feel to be an heiress?" he asked.

Peggy stirred her coffee thoughtfully. "I'm still too dazed to realize it. However, I haven't got the money. Uncle Giles will probably live for many years and I hope he does. I don't need his wealth. It was just his thoughtfulness that stunned me. It was so unlike him."

"Thoughtfulness?" Ted's tone was skeptical. "Why, you're the only one he has to leave his cash to. He didn't even have to make a will and you'd get it. It's my opinion he just made that will and had you down to hear about it so he could get a big feeling of generosity without its costing him anything."

"Ted!" Peggy was reproachful.

"I'm sorry, dear," he murmured. And then to change the subject, "You and your uncle are the last of the line."

"The last of the Delcarns," she repeated, half sadly. "And I'm the last of the Stonehams, too. That was my mother's name. She had one brother—my Uncle Bill—but I just vaguely remember him."

"What became of him?"

"He died somewhere out west, I believe. He used to visit us once in a while before mother died, but that was ten years ago, so my recollection's rather hazy. I only recall him as a big, blustery man who used to pick me up and toss me high in the air."

Ted nodded. "Well, Peggy dear, now that you're the last of the Delcarns, I suggest we ought to start a new dynasty. As long as you have Uncle Giles' fortune in prospect I suppose your objection to marrying a rich young man has been overcome."

"I have no objection of marrying a man with money," Peggy corrected him. "I only object to marrying a rich—loafer," she added, her brown eyes smiling but firm.

"I see. No work, no wedding—" He broke off suddenly.

"What's the matter?"

"Why—a—nothing," Ted said hastily, but he kept his eyes on the doorway across the dance floor, through which he had a narrow view of the entrance hallway of the inn.

"You look as though you'd seen a ghost. What is it—Ted!" Peggy sounded alarmed.

He turned back to her with a shrug. "Really, it was nothing," he insisted.

"I only saw someone familiar."

"What do you mean?" Peggy demanded.

Ted hesitated. There was no use to worry her unduly over what must be, after all, a mere coincidence. But he knew he'd have to make some explanation, so he told her about the wolf-faced man in the drugstore, who had listened to his telephone conversation.

"I'm sure I just saw him come in here," Ted added.

Peggy laughed with relief. "Heavens, is that all. Why, silly, of course, he listened to your conversation, but when you said you were going to the Wildfire Inn that gave him an idea. He was probably just making a date with his girl and he decided to take her here."

"Sure, that's it," Ted said in apparent agreement.

But he was far from feeling certain Peggy's explanation was correct. His mind ran back rapidly over the afternoon. The theft of the roadster, the obvious desire of the wolf-faced man to hear his phone conversation. And, above all, the sensation that was constantly growing on him that Peggy and he were being watched.

"Come on, Peggy. How about a dance?" he exclaimed, rising as the music broke into a hot number. No need to make Peggy share his nervous imaginings, Ted decided.

At eleven-thirty Peggy announced that she was ready to start for home.

"It's been a wonderful evening, Ted," she declared. "That's a dandy orchestra. I've almost danced my feet away."

They found Batt asleep behind the wheel of the big closed car. He awoke with an embarrassed start, when Ted touched him on the arm.

"Just catching forty winks," the chauffeur apologized as he got out hurriedly and held the car door open for them.

Peggy stepped in quickly and settled herself on the cushions, but Ted, pushing the door almost closed so she wouldn't overhear, stopped to speak to Batt. His voice was quiet. The other, however, familiar with his employer's moods, knew that he was concerned.

"I'm not easily alarmed as you know," Ted said softly. "But I've a hunch that we're being shadowed. You and I know I'd be good pickings for some of these blackmail and kidnapping gangs. So don't stop for anything on the way to Miss Delcarn's apartment."

"I got you, Mr. Trask. And I think you've got the right dope. Nobody's going to stop us."

"Good! I know I can count on you," Ted said. "It's only because Miss Delcarn is with us that I'm at all anxious. If you and I were alone, I'd say to hell with them. The more and tougher, the merrier."

He opened the door and joined Peggy in the back of the car. Batt touched his cap and took his place in the driver's seat. A second later the big motor roared away from the inn and down the Merrick Road toward New York.

"What's all the big conference about?" Peggy asked as she nestled closer to him.

"I was giving him his instructions—for tomorrow," Ted replied easily.

As they rolled rapidly along, Batt's eyes missed nothing that might have been regarded as suspicious. Every car they passed was looked over sharply and from time to time he glanced in the rear-view mirror, which extended out from the windshield.

The former prize-fighter had been born and reared in the lower East Side. He knew the full significance of what Ted had hinted at. And this was not the first time it had occurred to him that his easygoing and wealthy employer might appeal to some of the city's gorillas as a likely prospect for a shakedown.

Batt smiled quietly to himself. Unknown to Ted, he had taken precautions to be able to protect the man who had befriended him. Inside his neatly fitting chauffeur's blouse rested a flat black automatic. In his pocketbook alongside the chauffeur's license was a permit to carry it, issued by the police commissioner.

To neither Ted nor his driver had it occurred that Peggy Delcarn might be the object of a sinister attention.

They left the more sparsely settled part of the island and passed the city limits. Ted began to breath easier. Peggy, tired from a strenuous evening of dancing, had failed to notice his tenseness. When, at last, Batt brought the car to a stop before the door of the graystone house, Ted relaxed.

He assisted Peggy from the car and walked to the door with her. Batt stood quietly by the motor, but his glance roamed up and down the deserted street.

"Oh, Ted," Peggy said suddenly, as he was bidding her good night, "be a darling and mail some letters for me. I meant to bring them out before, but I was too excited over how you'd like my new dress."

"Sure," Ted replied.

She unlocked the door of the house. "You won't have to bother coming up. Just stand inside and I'll toss them down the stairs."

Peggy pulled his head down and kissed him. Then she turned and ran lightly up the stairs. Ted waited, holding the wide front door of the house open. His eyes, filled with admiration and happiness, followed her as her twinkling heels disappeared around the landing.

An instant later he let go the door and sprang up the stairway three steps at a time. Batt, too, had galvanized into action. Before the door had clicked shut, he was inside the hallway and, automatic in hand, followed Ted.

From above had come a startled scream!

V

A GRUESOME DISCOVERY

"TED! TED!" THERE WAS ALARM AND HORROR IN PEGGY'S VOICE.

"What's wrong?" he demanded breathlessly, taking the last few steps at a bound.

Peggy was leaning against the frame of the open door to her apartment. One hand was clasped at her breast; with the other she pointed unsteadily to the floor inside.

The lights were on and through the open doorway Ted saw the figure of a man stretched out at full length.

With Peggy clinging to him, he entered the apartment. Batt, realizing there was no immediate need for his gun, slipped it back into his shoulder holster and followed them. He closed the door behind him.

The man on the floor was lying face down. One arm reached out straight, the other was doubled under him. Ted noticed that the edge of the rug was dragged up, as if the fellow might have tripped over it.

"I saw—it—the minute I switched on the lights," Peggy explained. "I—I couldn't help the scream," she added, almost apologetically.

"Of course not, dear," Ted replied reassuringly.

Batt walked to the man and turned him over. Peggy covered her face with her hands. Ted gasped.

The contorted face and glassy, staring eyes left no doubt that the fellow was dead. The hand which had been doubled underneath, Ted saw, clutched a small flashlight.

"A burglar, it looks like," Batt suggested.

"Probably," Ted agreed. He thought a minute. "Well, I guess there's nothing to do but notify the police."

By this time Peggy had recovered from the first shock of finding the body. Her voice was well under control when she spoke.

"The telephone's in the next room. Come, I'll show you where the light switch is."

When he hung up the receiver after calling the station house, Ted turned to her.

"You can't stay here tonight," he said firmly.

She shook her head. "I'm no coward, but the way I feel now I wouldn't stay in this apartment alone for another minute. I'd better get a room at a hotel, or I might go and bunk in with Adele Gale."

"It's too late to wake her up," Ted said. "No, the thing to do is to come right out to my place. Oh, it'll be quite proper," he added quickly. "Aunt Lucy's there. She'll be delighted to have you."

"I suppose that is the best plan," Peggy admitted after a little hesitation. "I'll get my things together." She brought a small overnight bag from a closet and began to pack, while Ted joined Batt in the room where the body lay.

"What do you make of that?" the chauffeur asked, pointing to the rug with the tip of his shoe at a point close to the outstretched hand of the dead man.

Ted followed the movement with his eyes. On the dark rug he saw a whitish stain about the size of a quarter. Near it were several pieces of broken glass.

Dropping on one knee to look more closely, he noticed that the fragments were curved, as if they once had formed a fragile cylinder.

"Looks a little like the broken lenses of eyeglasses," Ted ventured. "But I don't see the bridge anywhere." He stood up and stared down at the dead man.

The body was dressed in a dark suit of good quality, a white soft shirt and a tie of subdued shade. The face, Ted saw, was young and inclined to swarthiness, which the pallor of death had not entirely obliterated.

"It's my idea," Batt said, "that this fellow came in here to rob the place. He was scared anyway and when he tripped over that rug it was too much for his ticker."

Ted nodded agreement. "That's about the way it strikes me, Batt. He died of a heart attack while committing a burglary."

The buzzer of the front door rang imperatively. Ted crossed and pressed the button which unlatched the lower door.

"Here are the police now," he said.

He admitted two plainclothes men, both large individuals with soft hats pulled down in front.

"What's the matter here?" one of them demanded.

Ted pointed to the body. "We came home and found that lying on the floor."

The other police officer stooped over and examined the figure on the floor. "He's dead."

"Yes," Ted agreed dryly. "We ascertained that. He's dead. Quite dead."

"You the party who phoned in about this?" the first plainclothes man asked.

"Yes."

The officer pulled out a notebook. "Tell us what you know about it."

"My name is Trask—Theodore Trask," Ted said, handing him a card. "This is my chauffeur—and this is Miss Delcarn," he added, as Peggy, attracted by the voices, came from the other room. "This is her apartment."

In as few words as possible he related how they had returned from an evening at the Wildfire Inn to make the gruesome discovery. The plainclothes man made numerous entries in his notebook during the recital.

"The body is just where we—that is, Miss Delcarn—first saw it," Ted said, "except that we turned it over before we knew the man was dead."

"Any of you know this guy?"

"No. None of us ever saw him before." Ted indicated the flashlight. "That led us to believe he was a burglar. We didn't notice any wound on him, so we imagined he might have had a heart attack while robbing the apartment."

The second plainclothes man spoke up. "That's right, Joe," he said. "There isn't a mark on him. And there isn't a thing in his pockets to show who he is."

Peggy had walked to where Ted was standing and was holding his arm lightly.

"Will we—do we have to stay here long?" she asked, a trace of anxiety in her voice. "It's rather harrowing to look at. I—I'm a little upset about it." She smiled wanly.

The officer deliberated. "Well, lady," he said finally, "I'm afraid you'll have to stay until the medical examiner comes. If he says it's like your friend believes—that this guy died from natural causes—you probably can go and if we want to question you any more, we'll send for you to come to the station."

"And if the medical examiner decides there is anything suspicious about this fellow's death?" Ted asked.

The policeman shrugged his shoulders. "I'm afraid you'll all have to go to the station. Then it's up to the lieutenant."

"We might as well sit down and take it easy," Ted said. He realized the futility of argument.

The two plainclothes men began a thorough search of the apartment. The one with the notebook asked a number of routine questions from time to time, the answers to which he duly entered.

A short time later the buzzing of the door bell announced the arrival of the assistant medical examiner. He was a young doctor, somewhat bored with proceedings.

The police officer with the notebook explained the circumstances and the examiner bent over the body. A little later he straightened up.

"Heart attack," he said briefly. "Take him to the morgue to await identification."

"I guess you folks can go then," the policeman said. "I've got your names and it may be necessary for you to come in for some more questioning, but I don't think so."

"We'll be glad to, of course," Ted replied. "Much obliged, officer, for your courtesy."

He brought Peggy's bag from the other room. "You'll see that the door is locked after you're through, won't you?" he asked.

"Sure," the policeman nodded.

As he assisted Peggy down the stairs, Batt following them, Ted thought of the broken glass and the stain on the floor. But what was the use of calling the attention of the officers to it. It probably meant nothing and would only result in their being obliged to go to the station, if the policemen decided it was significant.

In the car, Peggy let her head rest against Ted's shoulder. He slipped his arm around her.

"Poor kid," he murmured sympathetically. "Our happy evening had a horrible ending, didn't it?"

She sighed. "Oh, Teddy, wasn't it lucky you were waiting for those letters. I don't know what I should have done. When you're with me I feel so—safe."

The first faint streaks of dawn were beginning to appear, when Batt turned the big car off the public road and up the drive to the *porte-cochère* of the big house.

"Any orders for the morning, sir?" he asked Ted.

"No. We'll probably sleep until noon and you'd better do the same."

While Peggy waited, Ted dug into his pocket for his latchkey.

"Someone else is staying out late," he remarked, as he turned the lock and swung the door open.

A black automobile was driving along the public road past the Trask estate. As it came opposite the house it seemed to slow down, then the driver put on more speed and it faded into the morning mists.

VI

Ominous Calm

The rambling white house, where ted lived with his spinster aunt, was not exactly one of the show places of that part of Long Island. But it was roomy and comfortable and the interior appointments were marked by perfect taste. It was the sort of home that a family whose wealth dated back several generations would have.

The grounds, however, were extensive, more than five acres, reaching from the road in front to a small cove off Long Island Sound in the rear.

About two acres, covered with woods, had been allowed to run wild. The remainder of the property was beautifully landscaped and carefully tended. A beach of white hard sand afforded ideal bathing. From the garage, which was at one side and a little back of the house, a path led down the gentle slope to a boathouse.

It was well after noon before Peggy and Ted sat down to what Aunt Lucy described as their breakfast and her luncheon. She had been awakened by Ted in the small hours of the morning to greet Peggy, but, as he had foretold, was delighted to have her there.

"My dear," she said to Peggy, while pouring the coffee, "I don't see how you ever managed to get through that awful ordeal!"

Peggy smiled wanly. "It was a case of *must* with me. But now I'm going to be obliged to get another apartment. I couldn't live there any more."

"Listen, Peggy," Ted suggested, "why don't you stay out here today and rest up? Then, tomorrow, we'll have Batt drive us in town and I'll help you look for a place. If we don't find what you want, you come right back out here with me."

"Yes, do, my dear. That's a very sensible plan," Aunt Lucy urged.

"Well—I'd really like to," Peggy said hesitantly. "And I suppose there's no reason why I can't, if you want me to do that."

"Great!" Ted exclaimed jubilantly. "That's settled. After luncheon we'll go for a ride in the speedboat and then take a swim."

They finished the meal and Peggy and Ted strolled across the velvety carpet of lawn to the boathouse.

"What a beauty!" she exclaimed excitedly, as they entered the low-eaved building and her eyes rested on the gleaming mahogany of a twenty-eight-foot speedboat.

"Wait till you see it travel," Ted said.

He stepped on the electric starter. A preliminary splutter and then the powerful motors caught with a roar. He throttled them down, pulled in the clutch and the rakish little craft glided smoothly into the channel that had been dug from shore to deep water.

"Why, it's just like driving your car out of the garage!" Peggy exclaimed delightedly.

Ted nodded and swung the wheel. They thundered out the entrance of the cove into the open sound. He threw the throttle wide and the shiny hull seemed to leap from the water. Two sheets of white spray on either side of the bow made it look like some giant gull skimming the surface.

Later, as they glided back into the boathouse, he knew by Peggy's glowing cheeks and shining eyes that he had managed to make her forget, if only temporarily, the horror of the night before. And the rest of the afternoon, too, he tried to drive painful thoughts from her mind with a swim and a run over to Port Washington for tea at a quaint old tearoom.

After dinner that night, Ted left Peggy and his aunt conversing on the south verandah and strolled out to the garage. He found Batt seated near the door to his living quarters, reading, not without some difficulty, a paper devoted to sports.

"Don't think I'm suffering from jumpy nerves, Batt," Ted said thoughtfully, "but the truth is, I'm a little worried about tonight."

"What do you mean, sir?" There was a puzzled look on the old fighter's face.

"Well, I can't exactly account for it, but after what happened last night, I've a strange sense of foreboding. Sort of a hunch that we may be in for trouble of some kind."

The chauffeur nodded understandingly. "Mr. Trask, I've got it, too. There's something fishy about that dead guy in Miss Delcarn's apartment."

"I was just wondering—" Ted began, and then fell silent, thoughtful.

"If this was only in New York, I'd get hold of my old friend, Tim McBride, and he'd send out a couple of men to guard the place," Batt said.

"Tim McBride?"

"Him and me grew up together as kids on the East Side," Batt explained. "Now he's a captain on the force and right next to the inspector in charge of detectives."

Ted smiled. "Well, that won't do us much good. But it's along the line I was thinking about. Do you know a couple of husky men I could get to patrol the grounds tonight? Just to be on the safe side."

Batt tossed his paper on the chair. "Mr. Trask, there's no need to get any outsiders. I'll do it myself. I've got a rod—a gun—and a permit, so there won't be any trouble if I should have to use it."

"I hate to ask you to do that, Batt. It isn't your work."

"I want to, Mr. Trask," the chauffeur insisted. "Nobody's goin' to come monkeyin' around here, if I have my say-so."

Ted seemed relieved. "I'd certainly appreciate it if you would keep your eye open. Tomorrow, if we go in town, I'll drive and you can make up your rest."

He returned to the verandah and joined Peggy and his aunt. The thought that Batt would be on guard lifted the ominous feeling from him somewhat.

Aunt Lucy tactfully bethought herself of an unperformed duty that required her attention indoors. Ted and Peggy sat on the steps of the verandah and talked. They seemed closer than ever before. He felt that somehow she had suddenly become dependent on him.

"Ted," she said, at last, "I think I'll go to bed. I'm tired out. I didn't get much sleep after last night."

He kissed her goodnight at the head of the stairs. She entered her room at the end of the hall at the front of the house, while he walked slowly to his room at the back overlooking the sound.

Until he got into bed, he didn't realize how tired he was also. But he stretched out luxuriously and then, settling his head into the pillow, dropped off to sleep almost at once.

The next thing he knew, he was sitting bolt upright in bed. He was wide awake, yet he could not have told what awakened him. Through the window he saw a full moon high in the sky. It must be after midnight, he thought vaguely.

Then he grew tense. He heard no sound except a dog baying in the distance. But Ted was vividly conscious of an alien presence—an indefinite sense of danger.

VII

IN THE NIGHT

TED SLIPPED SWIFTLY OUT OF BED. He pulled on his trousers and put his feet into a pair of sneakers. Silently he stepped to the window and looked out.

It was a calm cloudless night. The back part of the grounds, which came within the range of his vision, was flooded in moonlight. Under the trees and in the woods to the left, however, the shadows were intensified by the brightness of the open spaces.

He looked at the luminous dial of his wrist watch. Two o'clock.

For several minutes he stood there, tense and watchful. There was no movement on the lawn outside. Only a deadly silence. Then again from the distance came the mournful baying of the dog. From far off the faint sound of an automobile on the highway.

Imagination, Ted decided. His nerves, strained by the events of the last twenty-four hours, were tricking him. He was about to return to his bed, when suddenly that ominous sense of menace swept over him again, stronger than ever this time.

He glided to the door of his bedroom and opened it cautiously. The night light in the hall burned dimly. Stepping out, he made his way softly to the banister and looked over. There was no sound from below.

He walked toward the front of the house and Peggy's room. With a start, he saw that her door was slightly ajar. At that same moment, there came from beyond the portal a cry of terror.

"Ted!"

In a flash he had burst into the room. Bending over the bed was a huge black form. Ted had a hazy impression that Peggy was beating frantically at the sinister figure, but at that instant he catapulted himself upon the marauder.

The two bodies came together with a crash. Ted, his arms around the giant figure, could feel that his clothes were wringing wet. Then the other staggered back and with a snarl shook loose his hold.

He was dealing with a man of superhuman strength, Ted realized. He stepped aside to the open part of the room, where he would not be hindered by furniture. In the moonlight, he caught a glimpse of a beastlike face, as the other, head jutting forward, came toward him.

Ted sidestepped and his right arm shot out. There was a crack as his fist met the jaw of his enemy. The ugly head snapped back, but with another beastly snarl the giant came on.

Left—right! Ted's arms were shooting like pistons. Every blow would have dropped an ordinary man in his tracks. But they seemed only to enrage this animal in human form.

Then the long arms closed about him and Ted was hurled violently back against the wall. He dropped to the floor. For a second, he was dazed. Picking himself up, he saw the huge figure climbing through the window to the roof of the verandah.

"Peggy! Peggy!" Ted cried. "Are you hurt?"

"No—no," came a frightened reply from the bed.

His head cleared now, Ted sprang through the window. As he climbed along the sloping roof, the animal-man swung over the edge and dropped to the ground. Ted followed.

When he had regained his balance after landing in the soft turf, the giant was lumbering across the lawn toward the patch of woods. He was making surprising speed in spite of his awkward gait. But Ted Trask had covered the four-forty on the cinder track in forty-nine seconds. Every stride brought him closer to his quarry.

At the edge of the lawn, the giant seemed to realize his pursuer was overtaking him. He turned and faced him, a growl of fury issuing from his curling lips.

This time, however, the battle was in the open, where Ted's speed and skill could have full play. He had found the jaw of his foe impregnable. His attack would have to be differently executed, Ted decided.

In an easy crouch he awaited the advance of the giant. Snarling now like a cornered mad dog, the man came on. Ted feinted with his right. Involuntarily, the other ducked and Ted stepped forward. His left arm seemed scarcely to move, but there was a dull thud.

A look of amazement spread over the hideous face of the giant. His mouth opened and his long arms dropped limp and paralyzed at his side. Ted's left jab had landed flush on his solar plexus.

Dancing nimbly back like the skillful boxer he was, Ted prepared to deliver the finishing blow. A right to the same spot. He closed in. But he had neglected to allow for the slipperiness of the dew-covered grass.

Ted's feet shot out from under him. The next thing he knew he was seized around the waist and tossed through the air like a sack of grain. Then someone was helping him to his feet.

"Mr. Trask! Are you all right?" It was Batt's voice. To Ted, it seemed to come through a thick fog.

Then his head cleared and he answered. "Yes, I'm—I'm all right," he gasped. "Where did he go?"

"Into the woods," Batt said quickly. "I saw you chasing him, but I was way over on the other side of the grounds and couldn't get here any sooner."

From deep in the wooded patch they heard the sound of crashing underbrush.

"He's heading toward the shore!" Ted exclaimed. "Quick! This way!"

Batt at his heels, he ran along the edge of the trees toward the beach. The noise of crashing underbrush in the woods had ceased.

They paused for a moment to listen. Ted looked back and saw numerous windows lighted up. The commotion had apparently awakened his aunt and the servants. Suddenly he was filled with a cold rage toward the man who had eluded him.

"We've got to get him, Batt," he muttered between clenched teeth.

They continued on their way more slowly, coming presently to a little knoll that overlooked the cove. Ted seized the chauffeur by the arm.

"Look! There he is!"

In the water of the cove they could make out the head and arms of a man swimming. Farther off on the edge of the shadow cast by the trees of the other shore was the dark outline of a motorboat.

"Shall I take a shot at him?" Batt asked.

Ted shook his head. "He's too far away. It would just alarm Peggy and Aunt Lucy."

While he was speaking, they heard a motor start up and the boat moved slowly out toward the swimmer. In the moonlight, they could make out his figure as he pulled himself over the side.

Ted sprang into action. "Hurry!" he shouted. "We'll chase them!"

He ran across the lawn along the beach toward the boathouse. Batt, grasping Ted's meaning, followed, although not able to keep up with his swift-footed employer. When he entered the boathouse, Ted already had stepped on the starter and the engines were spluttering. Batt took his seat beside him as he raced the twin motors a few seconds and then yanked the clutch in.

The speedboat roared out of the boathouse and into the channel. Deep water and Ted swung the wheel. The speeding craft careened and then righted itself as he straightened out for the entrance to the cove, through which the other boat had disappeared.

They emerged into the open waters of the sound. Batt, who was standing up, raised his arm and pointed. Off the port bow, Ted could distinguish in the distance a dark blotch and below it a smaller patch of white—the churning wake of the craft they were pursuing.

He swung the wheel again and the speedboat responded instantly. As they settled down to the chase, Ted pushed the throttle open to the limit. The mighty engines roared in a higher pitch. The boat was making close to forty-five miles an hour, he estimated.

Little by little the gap of water between the two boats lessened. Five minutes later, he could make out the outline of the other craft and the huddled figures in it, although he was unable to see exactly how many there were.

"We're catching them!" Ted shouted. His words were lost in the thunder of the motors, but Batt saw his lips move and nodded in understanding.

The chauffeur reached under his arm and pulled forth the heavy automatic. At their present rate of speed it would only be a question of minutes before they were alongside the other boat.

Suddenly from the craft ahead came a flash, quickly followed by two others. Batt fingered the pistol eagerly and looked at Ted, who was crouching low over the wheel, a grim set smile on his face. He shook his head. They would need all their cartridges in a little while.

Now Ted could see that there were three men in the speedboat. One of them was at the stern bending over. Scarcely a hundred yards separated the racing craft.

Batt, unable longer to restrain himself, raised the automatic and fired at the stooping figure in the boat ahead. He straightened up, arms above his head, and then fell back. At the same moment, a dark object dropped into the foaming wake.

"I got him!" Batt shouted.

He raised the automatic again, but his finger never pressed the trigger.

Dead ahead a mountainous wall of water rose up. Ted saw it and swung the wheel hard starboard. It was too late. The speedboat was caught under the port bow. Like a cockleshell it was hurled out of the water, then came down on its side.

Ted felt himself flying through space. Next he was fighting to reach the surface of the sound.

A little ways off, ten-thousand dollars worth of steel and mahogany filled rapidly and sank in twenty fathoms of water.

With a gasp, Ted reached the air. He looked around, swimming easily. The craft they had been pursuing was barely visible, although the sound of its motors came clearly to his ears. Of his own boat, there was no sign except several of the buoyant cushions, which floated near him.

"Batt!" he called and again, "Batt!"

"Here, Mr. Trask!" came a spluttering reply.

Ted looked behind. Batt was paddling toward him, seemingly with difficulty. Ted seized one of the floating cushions and pushed another toward the chauffeur.

"What's the matter?" he asked. "Are you hurt?"

"Naw," Batt muttered. "But it's hard to swim with this heavy gun in my hand."

Ted, in spite of the seriousness of their predicament, could not restrain a smile.

"For God's sake, let it go!" he exclaimed. "They're not coming back after us. Anyway, the gun's probably useless now."

Batt let the automatic sink and seized the life-preserver cushion with both hands.

"They must have thrown some dynamite," Ted said.

"If you ask me, I think they dropped an ashcan overboard."

"A what?"

"Ashcan," Batt repeated. "That's what the gobs called them there depth bombs during the war."

That must have been what the man in the stern was doing—pushing a depth bomb overboard, Ted thought. It suddenly came to him that the dead man in Peggy's apartment and the attack in the bedroom a short time before were part of a well-organized plot against her.

"How far do you think we are from shore?" he asked. Now he was anxious to get back to Peggy, to be at her side to protect her from the next move the mysterious forces might make.

"Better than a mile," Batt replied.

"That's what I figure. Guess there's nothing to do but try to make it. We'd better hang onto our cushions, though."

They started swimming toward the Long Island shore, a dark line in the distance.

"There ought to be fishin' boats comin' out pretty soon," Batt said. "We may get picked up."

"Can't count on it," Ted answered grimly.

They paddled in silence. Ted's thoughts were racing. Why should anyone be seeking to harm little brown-eyed Peggy, he muttered to himself. But in the same breath, he was forced to admit that someone undoubtedly was. The huge man in the bedroom was not a casual marauder. He had come in a swift motorboat, prepared for a getaway.

Several times they saw the running lights of small boats in the distance. But they were too far off to hear the cries of the men in the water.

They continued to make their way slowly toward the land. Some time later, Batt called Ted's attention to a red and a green light off to the right.

"He ought to pass pretty close to us," the chauffeur said.

The boat came nearer and both men shouted at the top of their lungs. Apparently the lookout on this craft was keeping a better watch. The course of the oncoming boat was changed slightly and a few minutes later it drifted up to them with motor idling.

"What the hell!" a gruff voice exclaimed.

"Our boat sank," Ted explained as they were helped aboard.

Ted saw they had been rescued by a boat about forty feet long with a decked-over cabin forward and a long, open cockpit aft. The man who had addressed them in the water was a heavy-set, rough-looking customer with a cap pulled down on one side of his head.

"You was certainly in a hell of a fix," he ventured. "Go ahead, Jake!" he added, shouting to a second man, who stood at the wheel. The explosions of the engine increased and they began to move again.

A third man appeared from the cabin. "What we stoppin' for?" he demanded.

"Picked up a couple of guys floatin' around in the water!" the man with the cap explained.

These men weren't fishermen, Ted knew. There was none of that unmistakable odor about their boat. But he surmised what their occupation was.

"How about setting us ashore?" he asked. "We'll make it worth your while."

The man in the cap hesitated. "Well, I'll tell you, buddy, we was just headin' up the island on a little private business. But—where do you want to go?"

Ted explained that they wanted to be set ashore at the entrance to the cove, where there was deep water right up to the land. He dug in his pocket and pulled out a soggy roll of bills.

"There's pretty close to a hundred dollars there," Ted said. "It's pretty wet, but it'll dry out and be as good as ever. It's yours to get us ashore at the point."

The man in the cap, who apparently was skipper of the rum boat, grinned. "That makes it look a lot different, buddy!" he said, and shouted an order to the man at the wheel.

Their rescuers, after letting them off, disappeared with a wave of their hands and Ted and Batt made their way on foot around the edge of the cove.

The big white house was ablaze with lights when they got back. Batt headed for his quarters at the garage. Ted entered the side door of the house and in the lower hall ran into Aunt Lucy in a state of nervous agitation.

"I've been worried to death!" she exclaimed. "Good heavens, what has happened? You're all wet!"

"Just a little swim," Ted replied. "Where's Peggy?"

Her eyes opened wide. "P-p-peggy?" she stammered. Then her face paled and she began to wring her hands. "I—I thought she'd gone with you!"

VIII

A SEARCH AND A CLUE

"YOU MEAN YOU HAVEN'T SEEN PEGGY SINCE WE LEFT IN THE BOAT?" Ted laid his hand anxiously on Aunt Lucy's arm.

"I was awakened by a lot of noise in Peggy's room," she explained. "As soon as I could find a wrapper, I went to see what it was all about. I met Peggy in the hall. She had on her dress and shoes."

"She was dressed?"

Aunt Lucy nodded emphatically. "She told me that you had chased a burglar from her room and were hunting him on the grounds. She was going out to join you, she said, and seemed very much worried about you."

Ted's heart sank. He cursed himself inwardly for having gone off on the wild goose chase after the motorboat, leaving Peggy alone and defenseless.

"A few minutes later," his aunt was continuing, "I heard the speedboat leave, and I thought, of course, she was with you."

"Aunt Lucy," he said decisively, "have the servants search the house from cellar to attic! I'll get Batt and we'll go over the grounds!"

Batt was greatly concerned at the news of Peggy's disappearance.

"Wait'll I get my pants on and I'll be with you!" he told Ted, who was standing at the door to his quarters.

"Bring a flashlight!"

For half an hour they tramped over the estate, calling her name at frequent intervals. Batt, with the flashlight, led the way as they beat through the thickets of the wood lot. They found no sign of her.

It was growing light. A terrible fear had gripped Ted, a fear that was mixed with rage at his helplessness. When he spoke, his voice was strained.

"We'll walk along the hedge," he said, "and then I guess we'll have to give up the hunt here. I've a feeling they won't find her in the house."

They had gone only a short ways along the neatly trimmed hedge of box, when he suddenly darted forward. At the spot where the hedge, perfect in its symmetry everywhere else, had been crushed down and broken, he stopped.

"Was this place here yesterday?" he asked sharply.

Batt hesitated. "Well, Mr. Trask, I couldn't say for sure. But I don't think so. You know how proud the gardener is of that hedge. He watches it like a hawk.

He'd probably have put a wire to protect it while it was growing again."

Ted pushed his way through the broken greenery to the road. He began to examine the ground and a few seconds later gave a shout.

"Batt!"

The chauffeur joined him. In his hand Ted held a small woman's slipper of reptile skin. Batt looked at him inquiringly and he nodded.

"It's Peggy's. I noticed them last evening." There was a catch in his voice. But immediately he became brisk and determined.

"It's a little after five," he said, consulting his watch. "You go back and catch a couple of hours' sleep. Then we're going into New York. Do you think you can carry on with that amount of rest?"

"Listen, Mr. Trask," Batt replied earnestly, "you know I'm going to see this thing through in spite of hell. Not only for your sake, but also because of Miss Delcarn."

They shook hands silently.

"Thanks, Batt," Ted said simply. "I knew I could count on you. By the way, you mentioned a Captain McBride on the police force last night—"

"An old buddy of mine," Batt nodded. "We grew up together. Now he's a big shot at headquarters. Right next to the inspector in charge of the dicks."

"Good!" Ted exclaimed. "I think we'll drop in to see him. It's reached a point where we've got to let the police take a hand with us."

"He's a swell guy," the chauffeur said. "I know he'll do all he can to help."

They walked slowly across the lawn, Ted turning the slipper over and over in his hand. He entered the house, while Batt made his way to his own quarters to obtain a short sleep.

"Where is Aunt Lucy, Celeste?" Ted asked, catching sight of the maid in the lower hall.

"She's in the breakfast room, sir. Oh, what a terrible night this has been, Mr. Trask!" she added.

He found his aunt, pale and frightened, sitting at the table. She was drinking a cup of coffee and urged him to join her. While she poured it for him, he sat gazing out the windows of the breakfast room.

"You found no trace of her in the house?"

Aunt Lucy shook her head sadly. "No. The servants went over it thoroughly. Her room has just been made up. It was very dirty. The burglar had tracked mud all over."

"Are you sure she went out after you talked to her last night?" Ted was grasping at straws.

"I'm positive, Ted," his aunt replied. "And I'm sure she didn't come back in. I was downstairs watching, because I was worried about you."

• • •

He gulped his coffee and, excusing himself, left the breakfast room, going from there to the library.

Somewhere in the house a telephone jangled. Ted pulled out a cigarette and stood listening. A minute later, Celeste appeared in the doorway.

"You're wanted on the phone, Mr. Trask."

Hope flamed in his breast. Perhaps it was Peggy! With a quick stride he crossed to the desk and picked up the extension telephone instrument. He lifted the receiver.

"Hello!" There was no answer. "Hello! Hello!" he repeated impatiently.

He thought he heard a faint click. Again he spoke, more loudly, but still there was no reply. He began to jiggle the hook. Presently, the voice of the operator, cool and impersonal, came to him.

"Number, please!"

"I'm not making a call, operator!" he exclaimed with annoyance. "Someone called me. But there doesn't seem to be anyone on the line now."

"Will you hang up, please, and let them call you again."

"That's the trouble. I'm afraid they won't. Can't you trace the call for me. This is Mr. Trask at Port Washington 0055."

The operator appeared to hesitate. Then she said, "Just a minute, please."

With increasing restlessness, he waited. Could it have been Peggy trying to reach him? Again the operator's voice came over the wire, crisp and businesslike.

"The call to Port Washington 0055 came over a New York circuit. We cannot trace it beyond that."

"Are you sure?" he asked.

"Yes, sir."

There was a note of finality in her tone. He thanked her and hung up the receiver. There was nothing to do but wait in hope that the call would be made once more. It came from New York. Now, who the devil? There were any number of persons who might telephone him; some of his college friends would even think early in the morning an excellent time. But he felt sure that the call, if not from Peggy, at least was connected in some way with her disappearance.

Fifteen minutes passed. There had been no further ringing of the phone and Ted reluctantly admitted to himself that the chances of his getting the call again were remote.

He was still in the clothes he was wearing when the depth bomb had capsized the speedboat. They had dried on him and he had been so disturbed over Peggy he had scarcely been conscious of how he was dressed. Now he decided he'd better go up and take a shower and change. It would be time to start for the city then.

While he shaved, he noticed that his face looked haggard and drawn. There were dark circles under his eyes and he knew that they were caused more by worry than loss of sleep.

A cold shower and fresh clothing, however, made him feel better physically at least. As he walked down the stairs, he met his aunt.

"Where are you going?" she asked.

"Into New York."

She took his arm and looked up at him. He saw that her eyes were red and tear-filled.

"Oh, Ted, I hope no harm comes to her! This is awful. The suspense. Who—who do you think is responsible for her disappearance?"

"I mean to find out," he said grimly. His usually smiling lips were set in a thin, dangerous line. He placed his arm around her reassuringly. "Don't worry, aunty. I'm going to get in touch with the police and they'll find her."

"I certainly hope so," she sighed.

Ted kissed her lightly and continued on down the stairs. He was far from feeling the confidence in the police that he pretended. If Peggy was to be rescued, he felt, Ted Trask would have to be the one who did it.

To his surprise, Batt was in the garage working over the big closed car. He grinned slightly at Ted's expression.

"Got to have the rolling stock in good shape," he said.

As they headed for the city, Batt at the wheel, a sudden horrible thought struck Ted—a thought that set his nerves tingling.

What if Peggy's abductors had seized her to take her for a ride in gangster fashion! To kill her in their car and then hurl her body out at some lonely roadside spot.

IX

MURDER

CAPTAIN TIM MCBRIDE RAISED HIS BUSHY GRAY BROWS thoughtfully. He chewed for a moment on his cigar, after which he let his gaze rest on his two visitors.

Batt's prophecy that the police official would be more than friendly had been fulfilled. McBride had greeted the old time pugilist with enthusiasm, and when he learned that Batt had brought Ted to him to get help, he expressed himself as eager to be of any assistance he could.

"It's an unusual story you've just told me," he said finally to Trask. "But, to tell you the fact, I'm not surprised at it."

He lapsed into silence, and, when he resumed a minute later, his voice was grave.

"For a couple of months now, we've had a suspicion that there's a gang of killers working in the city. Not ordinary killers, mind you," he added quickly, raising his finger meaningly, "but a mob of damned clever fiends. I don't know how else to describe them."

Ted was startled. "You—you think, perhaps, that Peggy—Miss Delcarn—has fallen into their clutches?"

The captain pursed his lips. "I'm only guessing," he replied. "This may be a simple case of kidnapping for ransom. But in view of the dead man you found in her apartment and the attack on her while she was sleeping, I doubt it.

"We've been trying to get a line on this sinister outfit for some time," the captain added, "but so far we haven't had a bit of luck."

"What do you advise me to do?" Ted's tone gave evidence of the mental tension he was under.

McBride considered. "Well, I'll put a couple of men on the case right away. There isn't anything for you to do that I can see, except you might inform Miss Delcarn's uncle of her disappearance."

"When we met him in his office day before yesterday, he said he was going out of town. However, he may be back now," Ted replied. "I agree with you that he should be told. He's her only relative."

He stood up and put out his hand. "I appreciate the interest you're taking in this matter."

The captain smiled reassuringly. "That's my business, Mr. Trask. If this is a ransom mob we're dealing with, you'll probably hear from them pretty quickly. Let me know at once if you get any message."

As he and Batt left the police headquarters, Ted noticed that it was shortly after nine o'clock. If Delcarn had returned to town, he decided, he might be in his office now. He directed Batt to drive to the building on William Street, where Peggy had taken him to meet her uncle.

Riding up in the elevator to the tenth floor, he thought with a pang of the other time he had made the trip. Then little Peggy had been with him. They had laughed and joked. The world had seemed a gay and carefree place. Now . . . Ted set his jaw.

Old Delcarn would probably get very excited, Ted imagined. He had seemed like the sort of person who would lose his head in a critical moment. Probably would want to set a flock of private detectives on the trail. Well, that might be a good plan, but Ted held the belief that it would be wasted energy.

In front of the door at the end of the hall, he paused. Through the frosted glass panel, he saw the shadow of a man sitting at the desk. Either Delcarn had returned or someone else was using his office.

For a second, Ted hesitated whether to knock or walk right in. At that instant he heard a sound that caused him to swing the door wide and leap into the office. It was an exclamation of surprise, followed by a low moan.

Delcarn was at the desk, but he was bent over with his head resting on the top and his arms spread out. Stooping over him was a young and sallow-faced man.

At Ted's entry, the fellow straightened up, at the same time withdrawing from between Delcarn's shoulder blades a dripping red stiletto. He let out an oath and half turned toward the open window. Then, as if realizing he was trapped, he made for Ted, the murderous weapon raised.

His first shock of horror over, Ted had already started for the killer. The wicked-looking blade swished through the air at the same moment Ted Trask's fist shot out. There was a rip of cloth and he felt a stinging sensation in his arm.

His foe, however, had avoided Ted's blow by parrying it with the dagger. Now he sprang back and crouched, his cruel face distorted with hate.

Once more they closed. Once more Ted's nimble adversary slashed and leaped aside from the fist. Ted realized that he was dealing with a skilled knife fighter. He dared not throw caution aside and rush him. It was bare knuckles against steel.

This time the man with the stiletto backed against the side. He put one hand behind him and braced it against the wall, preparing for a leap that would break through Ted's flying fists.

Like a panther he sprang. Ted's feet moved as gracefully as those of a toe dancer. He sidestepped. The dagger flashed, but Ted was not there. He crossed a right that had all the power of his hundred and ninety pounds behind it.

The man with the knife was lifted off his feet. While he was still in the air, Ted's left caught him on the jaw with bone-crushing force. He was hurtled through space, landing in a limp heap in a corner of the office.

Ted was after him in a flash. But he saw that his foe was out completely. He lay helpless, his deadly knife on the floor beside him.

"We won't risk any chances with you!" Ted gritted out.

Swiftly he took the man's necktie and bound his ankles. Then with his silk handkerchief he fastened his wrists behind him and rolled him against the wall.

He turned his attention next to Delcarn. A great red splotch on his back was widening rapidly. On the floor beneath the chair was a pool of blood. A quick examination convinced Ted that Delcarn was beyond human aid. The thin blade of the stiletto had pierced his heart.

The murdered man, apparently, had been writing at the desk when he was attacked. A fountain pen was clutched in his lifeless fingers. On the desk, smeared with blood, was a crumpled sheet of paper.

Ted picked it up and ran his eyes over it quickly. Then he gave a low whistle and put it in his pocket.

It was more necessary than ever that he lose no time now!

In the hall outside, several other figures were visible. Ted decided that it was only a question of a few minutes before they would get the building superintendent to admit them, probably with the police.

His only chance was by way of the window. He walked over and glanced out and down. The areaway was about ten feet wide, he saw, bounded on the far side by the wall of the adjoining building. There was no fire escape that he could possibly make his way down, and for a second Ted's heart sank. He would have to go out the door and face the music.

Then he noticed that floors of the other building were on different levels from the one he was in. Directly across and a half a story down was an open window, the sash lowered from the top. The partial view he had through it, showed him that the room beyond was a washroom.

He climbed through the window and stood poised on the sill. He dared not look down. He was ten stories above the street. A quick glance behind revealed that the persons in the hall were preparing to unlock the door. It was now or never.

His eyes glued on the window across the way, Ted crouched. Then he hurled himself into the air.

His feet found the ledge and his arm hooked over the open window sash. For a second his grip slipped, and his heart stood still. It was certain death if he fell. Then his steel muscles tightened their hold and he scrambled through the opening to safety.

A few minutes later, Batt looked up in surprise to see his employer approach, his clothing disheveled and the sleeve of his gray coat stained crimson from the stiletto wound in his arm.

Ted jumped into the car and slammed the door.

"Back to police headquarters!" he exclaimed. "And step on it!"

X

TRAPPED

LETHERIUS WAS STRIDING BACK AND FORTH ACROSS THE BIG ROOM. His hunched shoulders seemed more bowed than ever. But his red eyes were glowing and the two feverish spots on his ghostly cheeks were sharply visible.

Bonwix was sitting. He was as meticulously dressed as ever, the gardenia sticking jauntily from his lapel. His gray eyes with the pink lids, however, held a worried look, and he let his gaze rest on the mastermind of the murder company nervously.

"Well, at least we've got the girl!" Letherius spoke with chill triumph. He continued his pacing in silence.

The porcine business agent touched a match to his cigar, which had gone out, and his pudgy fingers shook almost imperceptibly. But Letherius noticed it and spoke sneeringly.

"My dear Bonwix, are you getting chicken-hearted?"

The fat man struck another match. Not until he was sure he had a light this time did he answer. When he did, his voice was steady.

"Chicken-hearted? Certainly not! It's just that this job has not—well, it hasn't gone as smoothly as all our others."

"You fool!" Letherius snarled out the words. "What's the matter with it? We've got the girl! We've got the money! Tonight I'll dispose of her, and wind up the deal in a businesslike manner."

"You mean—"

"I mean that my assistants seem to be a lot of blundering idiots, so I shall murder her myself and dispose of the body." His tone was coldly impersonal, like that of the head of any commercial firm who had decided to step in and correct the errors of his subordinates.

"It was too bad about Jenks," Bonwix said. "Just what happened?"

"He got what he deserved," Letherius responded heartlessly. "In other lines, failure is apt to mean the poorhouse. In our work, as you must understand, it's likely to mean the death-house!"

He laughed softly, grimly, but his jest evoked no response from the business agent.

"Jenks," Letherius continued, "did very well to start. He was smart enough to steal the roadster and hide it up in Harlem, because he realized that it was so speedy it would make difficult, if not impossible, a successful trailing of them. It's at the bottom of the East River now," he added.

"But how did Jenks happen to lose his life?" Bonwix asked. "I just know that he did."

"His own carelessness!" snapped the master killer. "While he let the Wolf trail the girl and this young Trask, he went to her apartment to plant the thin glass phial of poison as I had directed. He knew how fragile it was. He knew how deadly the formula was. But the fool broke it in his hand. We're well rid of him."

Bonwix stole a covert glance at his superior. The big man was just as conscienceless as Letherius. But he lacked the fiendish courage and resourcefulness of the smaller man and as he watched him stride back and forth, his eyes blazing redly, he began to regret the alliance he had formed with him, even though it had been profitable beyond all expectations.

Letherius resumed talking, almost a soliloquy.

"Against my better business judgment, I sent the Strangler out there. He, too, failed. Thank God, he got a bullet through his dumb skull!"

"Well, you were smart enough to be prepared, in case anything went wrong," Bonwix said soothingly.

Letherius nodded. "That's true. But it was only a lucky chance that she should have ventured out of the house alone, so the others in the car could seize her. But we have her now and tonight . . . Delcarn is on his way back from Detroit! Did you know that?" he asked suddenly.

The business agent looked surprised.

"I had a code wire from Mortboy. He didn't give any reason for his coming back so soon. Probably didn't know. But Mortboy's trailing him, and Mortboy is not such a fool as Jenks. The wire was sent last night. They should have arrived today. I'm waiting for a report now."

Letherius stopped suddenly and stared thoughtfully at the business agent.

"Do you think we have anything to fear from Delcarn? That he might—"

"Not a chance!" Bonwix interrupted. "We've never had a client who seemed so anxious for a deal to go through. Why, even before I gave him his instructions about leaving the city, he told me he was already taking steps for an alibi."

"What steps?"

"He said he was having his niece come to his office that afternoon to inform her he was making a new will in her favor. He would have witnesses to it. The whole idea was to show in what high regard he held her."

Bonwix laughed brutally. "The old fox knew she would never survive him. It was a perfectly safe move."

"A clever method of diverting suspicion," Letherius said appreciatively. "We must remember it."

"How about this fellow Trask?" Bonwix asked suddenly.

His superior snapped his long fingers. "A youngster. I checked up on him through a blind phone call early this morning. More than two hours after we had the girl, he was still at his house. He moves too slowly to cause us any annoyance from now on. He may go to the police—probably will—but they won't get anywhere," he added dryly. "However, if he becomes a nuisance—" Letherius left the sentence unfinished.

He took out his watch. "Eight o'clock! I believe that midnight would be the best time to take care of the girl." He uttered that weird macabre laugh. "Midnight—yes, my dear Bonwix, a very appropriate hour!"

The business agent repressed a shudder. The thought of the fiendish crime Letherius was soon to commit left him unmoved. But the unearthly laugh never failed to send chills up and down his spine.

"I'll be on my way," he said. He put his bowler hat on his head at a jaunty angle and adjusted his cravat. "I have an important engagement a little later."

Letherius raised his brows.

"No, it's a matter of business—our business. I am meeting a new client to conduct the preliminary negotiations."

The cadaverous killer rubbed his hands together briskly. "That is excellent, my dear Bonwix. Always after business! We will have this Delcarn deal cleaned up tonight and—well, the devil will find work for idle hands, I've heard it said." He let out a sinister chuckle. "But watch your step. Always be careful. I would really hate to lose your valuable services."

He pressed the button beside the desk and almost at once the silent-footed little Malay servant appeared.

"You will kindly show Mr. Bonwix out, Ko," he said softly.

After the portly figure of the other man had disappeared through the door, Letherius stood rapt in thought for several minutes. His eyes were shielded behind his long soft lashes. Then he bit his bloodless lips gently and murmured with a low tone of eager relish.

"Midnight! Ah, yes, at midnight!"

Bonwix, outside, hailed a taxicab and gave the driver an address in the uptown district. As he settled back in the seat, he, too, muttered to himself. But his words were of entirely different significance.

"If this proposition is to rub out a woman—nothing doing," he said. "It's too risky. Although I kind of think Letherius enjoys it."

The taxicab made slow progress through the Times Square district, but after passing Columbus Circle the traffic lessened, and presently the driver halted in front of a tall apartment house on West End Avenue.

Bonwix pulled out a large roll and peeled off a bill, which he handed to the cab man with a careless wave of his hand. Then he crossed the sidewalk with a dignified air and entered the lobby.

"Mr. William Easterly," he said to the attendant. "He's expecting me."

He waited patiently while the man announced him on the house phone. This was something like it, the business agent thought to himself. His prospective client certainly lived in a swell joint. He liked to do business with people who had class—and dough!

"Mr. Easterly wishes you to come right up. Apartment thirteen-nineteen. The elevators are this way, sir."

Bonwix stepped in and the cage shot up to the thirteenth floor. As he rang the bell, he wondered how Easterly had gotten his name and phone number. But that was the way it usually went. It was just a business deal, until he had talked to his prospects and they had satisfied him as to their reliability. Then, after some more investigation, it was time to get down to brass tacks—make the death pact.

He was admitted by a man servant and ushered into a spacious room.

"Mr. Easterly will be right in, sir," the man said, and departed from the room.

Bonwix took a seat and looked around him. He was more satisfied than ever that this was a likely looking proposition. Wonder who he wants bumped off? the business agent speculated. Well, he'd get an inkling pretty quick now.

Five minutes passed. Ten. Bonwix began to feel uneasy. What was keeping the man? He got up and walked around the room, looking at the several oil paintings that adorned the walls. He took out his watch. Minute by minute he became more convinced that something was wrong.

He walked to the door by which he had entered and turned the knob. It was locked! He pulled out his handkerchief and mopped his brow. He took his chair again, but he was unable to sit still. Something akin to panic was beginning to grip him.

A sudden click behind him caused the business agent to wheel in alarm. A second door at the far end of the room had opened. A tall military-looking man entered. His eyes were narrowed and he kept them fastened on Bonwix as he approached.

It was Police Captain McBride. Close on his heels were Ted Trask and Batt.

The fat man realized he was trapped. His gray eyes looked wildly about the room and his pink lids fluttered. Then he took refuge in bluster.

"See here, what's the idea of locking me in this room? I came here on a business appointment to see Mr. Easterly."

McBride's hand went out and his muscular fingers closed on the other's shoulder like a vice. He snapped the business agent back into his chair.

"Sit down!"

Bonwix sat, but his voice rose in a shaky protest.

"What's the meaning of this?"

McBride towered over him like a ruthless avenger.

"It means—you dirty rat—that we've caught you! You're going to talk, and if you don't—" He paused. His expression held a menace that would have thrown terror into a braver man than Bonwix. "I'm going to take the hide off you!"

XI

DEATH CALLS AGAIN

WHEN PEGGY DELCARN SAW TED CLIMB FROM HER BEDROOM and over the verandah roof in pursuit of the Strangler, she was filled with alarm for his safety. She hastened to the window. In the moonlight on the lawn, she could make out the two figures running toward the patch of woods.

Scrambling into her clothes, she made her way from the house, passing Aunt Lucy in the hall with a hurried word of explanation. Her one thought was of Ted as she hastened across the grounds. He was nowhere in sight.

When she neared a point where the woods and the road met, she was breathless, fighting off a sense of panic. Suddenly from beyond the hedge of box, two forms arose. Peggy turned to flee, but it was too late.

Before she could utter more than one small cry of fright, they were upon her. A heavy hand was pressed over her face and her hands were pinioned behind her. Then she was being carried, put into an automobile and the hand withdrawn from her face. But in its place she felt a damp cloth.

A sweetish, unpleasant odor filled her nostrils. Chloroform, she thought dimly. Then everything went black.

How much later it was that she recovered consciousness, Peggy was unable to determine. She opened her eyes with difficulty. The lids seemed to be weighted with lead and she was racked by a splitting headache. She raised her tortured body and looked around.

The room in which she found herself was small and sparsely furnished. Besides the cot on which she was lying, it contained only a single chair and a table. From one window, heavily barred, daylight penetrated.

She got up and made her way dizzily to the window. It was too small for her to get more than a fragmentary view outside, but the room in which she was imprisoned was high up, she noticed. Down the street, she caught a glimpse of a green park. Vaguely she imagined it looked like Gramercy Square.

A feeling of complete helplessness swept over her. She was no longer terrified; she was resigned to the horrible fate she felt must be in store for her. Where was Ted? What had happened to him? What had happened to her, for that matter?

She returned to the cot and lay down. Exhausted she fell asleep.

When she awoke, it was with the realization that someone was in the room. Turning her head, she saw a little brown-skinned man with slanting eyes. It was dark outside and the place was illuminated by a feebly glowing electric light in a wall bracket.

"Where—where am I?" she asked.

The man placed a tray of food he was carrying on the table and shook his head.

"Eat!"

Peggy sat up. "I don't want to eat!" The sound of her own voice gave her strength. "What—what am I doing here?" she demanded.

The slant-eyed man shrugged. "Eat!" he repeated cryptically and, opening the door, swiftly slipped out. A lock clicked.

She walked to the table and examined the food on the tray. But she was not hungry and a fear that it might be poisoned would have kept her from touching it, anyway. She drank a glass of water and then sat down. Black despair filled her heart.

Hours later the door was opened again. Once more, the Malay servant entered. He motioned to her to precede him from the room, and, like an automaton, she obeyed.

As they walked down a long hallway and began to descend a flight of stairs, she had a reckless impulse to make a dash for freedom—to fight madly for her life. But she knew it was useless. She had no knowledge of the layout of this house of horror. Then, too, she had seen jammed through the sash of the little Malay a shining *kris*—a wicked-looking dagger with a serpentine blade.

Letherius rose with a mocking and sinister gallantry. He dismissed Ko with a wave of his hand.

"Ah, Miss Delcarn," he purred. "Please be seated."

"What do you want with me?" she faltered, as she dropped hopelessly into a large armchair.

"Let us say that I am entertaining this evening," he replied with a malevolent smile. "Do not be afraid. You are quite safe."

Peggy's instinct told her that he lied. She was far from safe, she understood perfectly well. And she was also powerless to help herself.

She looked at the ghastly white face of the man and an involuntary shudder passed over her. His red eyes with their soft curling lashes leered at her. He took out his watch, a thin platinum affair, on which diamonds sparkled.

"Ten minutes to twelve!" He stood up. "I am keeping you out late. But do not worry. It is only for a little while longer."

He walked slowly to the chair in which he was sitting. "Come," he said, "we may as well start!"

"Where are we going?" she demanded, leaping to her feet.

"Don't be frightened," Letherius said, attempting to take her arm.

She stepped back, an expression of loathing on her face.

"Don't touch me!" she screamed. "Don't touch me!"

His fingers closed on her shoulder. "You'll do as I say! I am Letherius!"

She stared wildly into his eyes, smoldering red, and all the strength seemed to leave her body, as if she were under an hypnotic spell.

Letherius, briskly efficient, led her unresisting from the room. Along a hallway, then down a flight of stairs. Another flight of stairs and they were in a large basement.

In the center of the subterranean room, Peggy saw vaguely, was what appeared to be a large steel box. A pipe led off at one side and numerous smaller pipes entered it at the base. At the near side was a door just sufficiently large for a person to enter by stooping.

Letherius threw the door open. "Enter!" he commanded.

She trembled violently, but there seemed left in her no power of resistance and she obeyed his bidding. As she stepped inside the almost dark space, she saw a small iron chair and sank limply into it.

The steel door clanged. Letherius put his eye to a tiny peephole in the center of it and peered in, and, although he could see nothing but blackness, he shook his head in apparent satisfaction.

Then he made a circuit of the contrivance, pausing from time to time to examine a valve or a lever. From a bench nearby he took a small urn, which he placed with care under a spout-like pipe at one corner of the strange machine.

"A machine age we live in," he muttered softly to himself. "What could be more fitting than that we commit machine murder in our business."

Out of his inhuman ingeniousness, he had contrived this lethal chamber and crematory. With complete disregard for the much greater mental torture he inflicted, Letherius was opposed to inflicting unnecessary physical agony. Rather than burn his victims alive, he killed them painlessly with lethal gas. Then the flame in the device was lighted. The terrific heat generated by the oxy-acetylene burners reduced the body to ashes, calcining even the skeleton—reducing it to a fine powder.

No one would ever be able to make anything out of a small urnful of ashes, which could be scattered to the four winds.

Slowly he began to turn a valve. There was a faint hissing. His eyes were glowing more fiercely now, even as the devilish contraption he was operating would glow when the fires were lighted. But his manner was precise, filled with deadly determination.

Above in the house was a muffled report. Then another.

Letherius, the monster of the most horrible enterprise ever conceived, was too engrossed in his fiendish task to notice. Little by little, he opened the valve wider.

The door at the head of the stairs burst open. Letherius, at the interruption, turned with a snarl, prepared to denounce whichever one of his subordinates had dared to interrupt him. Then, with snakelike swiftness, his hand moved toward his hip.

A shot rang out, the bullet clanging against the steel door behind him, and Letherius fired back. But his bullet was wild.

Ted Trask leaped down the steps. Behind him, Batt, smoking pistol in hand, dared not risk another shot for fear of hitting his employer.

But there was no need. Before the murder master could press the trigger again, Ted was upon him. The younger man's fist moved too fast for the eye to follow. There was a crack—as if someone had broken a board across his knee.

Letherius' head flew backward. His hideous eyes seemed about to pop out of their sockets. Then his head dropped limply forward. And as the dealer in death sagged to the floor, a livid purple color began to spread over his ghastly ashen face. Ted's blow had broken his neck!

In a flash, Ted swung wide the steel door of the lethal furnace and picked the unconscious form of Peggy up in his arms.

XII
DELCARN'S MOTIVE

MR. RAYMOND CRANE, OF CRANE, WILLIAMS AND CRANE, attorneys-at-law, looked up from the mass of papers on his desk, as Ted Trask entered his private office.

"You wish to see me?" he asked.

"I'm here on Miss Delcarn's account, Mr. Crane," Ted replied. "She's still feeling the effects of her harrowing experience, and so wasn't able to keep the appointment herself."

"Ah, yes," the lawyer replied. "Won't you sit down, Mr.—"

"Trask," Ted said. "I am Miss Delcarn's fiancé." This wasn't the strict truth, he admitted to himself, but it was very, very close to it.

"Well, there is really no great hurry about Miss Delcarn's coming in," Crane said. "It's just that we have been going over her late uncle's affairs, and, of course, under the terms of a recent will she is his beneficiary. Trask? Why, as I recall it, you witnessed the instrument."

Ted smiled. "That's right. Just a few days ago."

"An odd man, Delcarn. A very odd man," the lawyer said thoughtfully. "It was a shame that he should meet such an untimely end."

"I don't think so!" Ted's voice was grim.

Crane looked at him in surprise. "Why—what do you mean by that, Mr. Trask? Delcarn was brutally murdered!"

"Right. He was brutally murdered—by one of the gang he had hired to murder his niece!" Ted whipped out.

"What?"

"Mr. Crane," Ted said quietly, "I want to be sure that does not reach Peggy's ears. That is one reason I came in to see you—in case some word of the circumstances should reach you, I wanted to ask you not to mention it to her. She's suffered enough. Let her continue to think her Uncle Giles was just a peculiar old man who thought a great deal of her."

"Please explain yourself!" the attorney said coldly. "Mr. Delcarn was one of our clients!"

Ted smiled quietly. "I'm well aware of that. But, Mr. Crane, I was the man who discovered his murder and tied up the man who stabbed him to death—this fellow Mortboy, who's held by the police."

Briefly Ted told of the story of his adventure in Delcarn's office. Crane was frankly astonished.

"When he was killed," Ted continued, "he was in the act of making a complete confession. Apparently, from the tone of his letter, his conscience had got the best of him. But he thought it was too late to save her and, stricken with remorse, was about to commit suicide.

"His letter was not finished. But it contained the name of the man through whom he had made the arrangements to kill Peggy—his niece."

"By George!" Crane leaped to his feet. "That explains something that's been puzzling us!"

"What's that?"

"Two letters we found in Delcarn's safe. They were from a law firm in Oklahoma City. They were trying to locate her—to settle up the estate of William Stoneham. Stoneham was her uncle, and, from the correspondence, I gather he left well over a million. Oil money.

"What puzzled us," the attorney went on, "was that Delcarn had written them that he was trying to locate his niece, but did not know if she was even alive. Yet we knew that he was aware she was, and saw her at intervals."

"That clears up the one question that bothered me—why Giles Delcarn wished to have Peggy killed!" Ted exclaimed.

"It certainly does!" Crane replied. "She was Stoneham's only blood relative and as such would inherit his fortune. Delcarn was not related. Peggy's father married Stoneham's sister. But if Peggy died, Delcarn was her heir-at-law and would inherit the Stoneham fortune."

Ted shook his head sadly. "It's hard to realize to what lengths some people will go for money," he said.

"That was Delcarn's curse. He loved money more than anything in the world," Crane replied. "Indeed, his estate will amount to several hundred thousand—all of which goes to his niece. Then, too, we are checking up on the Stoneham estate, which will go to her."

After dinner that evening, Ted and Peggy strolled across the grounds of the Trask country place. When they came to the little knoll, from which they could look across the sound to the winking lights of the Connecticut shore, they stopped. For a time they stood in silence. At last, Ted spoke.

"Well, Peggy dear, you're wealthy now, so I suppose your objection to—"

She reached up and placed a finger on his lips. "Yes, Teddy, I still object to marrying a man who wants to loaf through life. And—and"—there was a little catch in her voice—"I do love you, too!"

"Stubborn little sweetheart!" Ted said with a smile.

"I know someone else who's stubborn," Peggy replied.

He laughed. "Well, dear, we can settle it all very easily right now."

"How?"

"You won't give in. I won't give in. But I'll say to you: Miss Delcarn, will you marry me? Then you say to me: Mr. Trask, will you quit being a lazy loafer and go to work? . . ."

"Yes."

"And we'll both answer at the same time," Ted grinned. "Miss Delcarn," he said, "will you marry me?" His arm went around her.

"Mr. Trask," Peggy said solemnly, "will you quit being one of the idle rich?"

And together they exclaimed: "Yes!"

OFF-TRAIL PUBLICATIONS
Specializing in the era of American pulp fiction

THE WEIRD DETECTIVE ADVENTURES OF WADE HAMMOND
By Paul Chadwick
Volume 1: 10 stories, 180 pages, $18
Volume 2: 10 stories, 172 pages, $18
Volume 3: 10 stories, 202 pages, $18
Volume 4: 9 stories, 232 pages, $18

> *The Wade Hammond stories complete in four volumes. In these chilling adventures, all from the classic 1930's pulps,* Detective-Dragnet *and* Ten Detective Aces, *freelance investigator Wade Hammond battles a series of weird enemies. Some of the best of 1930's pulp fiction.*

DOCTOR COFFIN: THE LIVING DEAD MAN
By Perley Poore Sheehan • Introduction by John Wooley
8 novelettes, 178 pages, $16

> *Weird stories from* Thrilling Detective, *1932-33. A former character actor who faked his own death, Doctor Coffin runs a string of mortuaries by night and fights crime at night. One of the strangest detective series.*

SUPER-DETECTIVE FLIP BOOK: TWO COMPLETE NOVELS
From the pulp *Super-Detective*:
"Legion of Robots" (November 1940) by Victor Rousseau • Introduction by John McMahan •• "Murder's Migrants" (March 1943) by Robert Leslie Bellem and W.T. Ballard • Introduction by John Wooley
2 short novels, 174 pages, $18

> Super-Detective *started as a Doc Savage-like adventure pulp, then changed format to hardboiled detective. The* Flip Book *features a novel from each of the two phases with intros exploring the historical background. Exciting!*

PULPWOOD DAYS: VOL 1: EDITORS YOU WANT TO KNOW
Edited by John Locke • 180 pages, $16

Numerous articles from the writers' magazines by and about pulp editors, with ample biographical profiles. Editors include: Frank E. Blackwell (Detective Story, Western Story), Ray Palmer (Amazing Stories, Fantastic Adventures), Robert A.W. Lowndes (Columbia Publications), Edwin Baird (Weird Tales, Detective Tales), and many more.

GANG PULP
Edited by John Locke • 19 stories, 294 pages, $24

Hardboiled stories of the criminal underworld from the first year (1929-30) of the gang pulps: Gangster Stories, Racketeer Stories, etc. These violent tales came under immediate censorship pressure; the history is explored in an in-depth essay. "A remarkable work of popular-culture scholarship"—Mystery Scene, Fall 2008.

THE GANGLAND SAGAS OF BIG NOSE SERRANO
Volume 1: DAMES, DICE AND THE DEVIL
Volume 2: HORSES, HOBOES AND HEROES
By Anatole Feldman • Introductions by Will Murray
Each: 4 novels, 266 pages, $20

The first two volumes (of three) of the Big Nose Serrano novels from Gangster Stories, 1930-32. Feldman was the best of the gang pulp authors, and Big Nose was his most inspired creation, the berserking king of Chicago gangsters.

THE CITY OF BAAL
By Charles Beadle • Introduction by John Locke
7 stories, 240 pages, $20

Authentic stories of African adventure from an author who had traveled the lands he wrote about. Lost cities, strange tribes, jungle magic. Six stories from Adventure *(1918-22) and one from* The Frontier *(1925).*

AMAZON STORIES: VOLUME 1: PEDRO & LOURENÇO
By Arthur O. Friel • Introduction by John Locke
10 stories, 222 pages, $18

Friel's first ten stories from Adventure *(1919-20), following the strange experiences of two Amazon Basin rubber workers as they explore the jungle. The best of pulp adventure fiction.*

THE OCEAN: 100TH ANNIVERSARY COLLECTION
Edited by John Locke
20 stories, 234 pages, $18

Munsey's The Ocean *(1907-08) was one of the first specialized pulps, a sea-story magazine. The best adventure stories are included here, along with 30+ pages of nonfiction material, a history of the pulp, and extensive author profiles.*

FROM GHOULS TO GANGSTERS:
THE CAREER OF ARTHUR B. REEVE
Edited by John Locke
Vol 1 (fiction): 21 stories, 264 pages, $20 • **Vol 2 (nonfic)**: 260 pages, $20

Reeve was the leading American detective-story writer of the early 20th Century, with his scientific detective, Craig Kennedy. The astonishing breadth of his career is explored for the first time here. Vol 1 includes a cross-sction of fiction from all phases of career, including many never-before-reprinted pulp stories. Vol 2 provides a 40-page biography; an extensive Art Gallery of cover repros, interior illos, ads, etc; a 75-page guide to Reeve's work in all media; and more. An "excellent piece of scholarship"—Mystery Scene, *Spring 2008.*

Shipping: $3.00 media mail; $6.00 priority
Check or MO to:
Off-Trail Publications
2036 Elkhorn Road, Castroville, CA 95012
Paypal: offtrail@redshift.com

www.ingramcontent.com/pod-product-compliance
Lightning Source LLC
Chambersburg PA
CBHW050821180626
46814CB00004B/1404